NOWHERE

BY
ANTONELLA RIVALTA

"Nowhere can man find a quieter or more untroubled retreat than in his own soul."- Marcus Aurelius

Prologue

A warm night was falling over Hollywood, and the city lights were coming to life, bright against the rapidly darkening sky.

Camille meandered slowly toward her apartment, so tired that more than once she accidentally tripped on the dirty sidewalk.

Not to mention that her mind was elsewhere.

I don't know how much longer I can take this grind, she thought, glancing at the message on her phone. *Maybe, soon, I won't have to.*

She pulled up a text box on her phone. *Which reminds me. I'd better start making arrangements for this weekend.*

She'd have to text her neighbor Trudy to check her mail and water her plants. She'd have to tell the superintendent at the complex she'd be gone. And then there was the matter of Lila, who couldn't be left alone a second…

Oh, there was so much to do.

But it would be so much better than the hell of her day-to-day office drudge.

Originally, she'd thought working as a costume designer's assistant for a new Netflix series would be a dream job. This was L.A., the city of dreams, after all. Maybe she'd been a sob story, a cautionary tale, stepping fresh-faced and naïve off that bus from Iowa, but she truly believed that when she set out for the West Coast, she was destined for big things.

But she'd been wrong. While every day on the set was hell because her boss, Judy, usually pulled her in a hundred different directions, today had been particularly rough. She'd been so busy working on the costumes for the male lead that she'd ordered the wrong materials for a new outfit that needed to be done for the female lead by the end of the week. And now, because of her mistake, they'd have to delay filming until next weekend.

Judy had been livid, yelling at Camille and creating a scene in front of the entire crew, calling her the worst assistant she'd ever had.

Camille pressed her lips together and cringed in frustration, remembering it. Then she looked at the message on her phone, and all of those feelings seemed to slip away. She smiled. *But I'm going to have the last laugh. She'll see.*

She hurried down the street, busy with tourists who still believed that Hollywood was a legendary area, and not the shithole it really was. She smiled. *It's okay. If things go your way, Camille, soon, you won't have to even work anymore. You'll be a very spoiled woman, living in the lap of luxury, and Judy can go shove it.*

And it was all because of the man she'd met a few months prior.

She almost giggled as the thought took form in her head: of her, lounging poolside, the man she loved next to her. All the people back in Iowa who said she'd never accomplish anything in her life, all her stupid coworkers who thought her a loser… Soon they would all see how wrong they were, and she would laugh in their faces.

Her lips curled now into a dimpled smile. It was thanks to those perfect dimples that she always gave the impression of being such an adorable, innocent girl, making a lot of men go completely crazy.

But she never really cared for that kind of men: simple and pathetic, with nothing to offer. Deep down, she always knew that she deserved better, and now that she'd finally found him, a man with a place in society, a man that most women only dreamed of, no mediocre man was going to have her.

With those gratifying thoughts in mind, she reached her apartment and, as soon as she stepped in, let her purse fall to the floor. She inhaled deeply the marvelous fragrance of lavender that she was obsessed with as Lila, her Pomeranian, came trotting to the door. She patted the little pup's head quickly before walking toward the bathroom, the sound of her ballerina flats echoing as she stepped lightly across the tile.

The place wasn't the best; it was impossibly tiny, with some cracks between the floor's tiles where crumbs always found refuge, making it impossible to clean. None of the appliances or fixtures seemed to work right, and the paint on the walls was old and dingy, like the walls of a prison. Not to mention that the air was heavy and smelled of dust because she was never able to open either of the windows in the living room.

But the move from Iowa had sapped a big part of her savings, and this dump was all she could afford at the moment. It didn't matter. She'd told herself time and time again to suck it up, because it was only temporary. One day she would do better.

And two hours ago, she'd received the text that told her she was right. That all of those years of holding out for the man of her dreams had paid off.

She looked at it once again, and her smile grew bigger. *Love… Santa Barbara? This weekend? My treat. You deserve to be treated like a princess.*

A princess. Yes, that was exactly what she deserved.

Finally she'd met a man who realized it. Well, many men had tried to woo her, but not one of them was up to her standards. But this man was different. Never before had she dated such a successful, confident man who had the means to make his way in the world, to take the country by storm and make a name for himself. And tomorrow, that man was taking her to Santa Barbara for a long, romantic weekend. It was simply a dream come true.

She sighed, fantasizing about spending every weekend in heavenly, exotic places all over the world, in the company of her rich prince charming. Places like Greece… She'd always wanted to visit there. Maybe he'd take her there next. Oh, how wonderful that would be!

She could just imagine her jealous friends and colleagues

constantly prodding her for juicy details about her extravagant life. And Judy? Judy would absolutely *die* once they made their relationship public.

She simply could not wait.

As she walked out of the bathroom toward her bedroom, she felt like she was flying. She even twirled in the middle of the room as she reached for another shirt to put in one of her giant suitcases. Her silky summer dress elegantly swirled around her long, thin legs as she spun, wondering if she should bring a tube dress. It was sexy, daring… yes. A confident man like him gave her confidence. *Stunning*, he'd say. He always called her that.

She couldn't believe that a simple girl like her had gotten so lucky to be noticed by a man like him. Truthfully, her life hadn't been that great until that point. A farm girl in Iowa, she'd done her best to bury the fact that she'd spent most of her teenage years milking cows and riding on tractors. When she'd arrived in California, she felt like a hick, like she'd never be able to fit in. But when she met him, everything changed. He made her feel special, like she belonged on his arm.

Now, she had him wrapped around her pretty little finger and would never let him go. She wasn't stupid. She knew women wanted him. How could they not? She was well aware of the predatory looks that women constantly threw at him. She even joked with him during their long afternoon trysts that every woman he came across wanted him. But he told her that he didn't care. *You're the only woman I want,* he'd said, gazing into her eyes before kissing her deeply, a kiss she felt straight to her toes.

Really, what else could she ask for?

Lila started barking, noticing her excitement. She grabbed her little white dog. "What's got you so riled, Baby?" she asked, kissing her and holding her tight in her arms, while the dog frantically wagged her small tail and licked her nose.

Lila whimpered, as if to say, *Don't leave me.*

Camille started laughing. "Aw, I wish I could take you with me, but my love isn't too fond of dogs, unfortunately. I guess we'll have to change his mind about it, won't we?"

The dog kept licking her nose, and Camille put her down, still laughing. She'd change his mind. After all, she was the only woman he wanted. Everything was going her way, falling into place even better than she'd hoped on that bus from dusty old Iowa.

Resting her hands on her hips, she studied her suitcases, open on the bed, half of her closet neatly folded inside. Was she forgetting anything?

She kept putting clothes, shoes and accessories in the suitcase and taking them out again, until she decided that it'd be totally fine to bring more than one. He'd probably tell her not to, that they weren't staying that long… or he'd wink and tell her he liked her better unclothed.

But he wouldn't get mad. She'd just use her dimples, and he'd let it go.

While Camille was trying to think about what she was missing, she heard a knock at the door. Lila sprinted toward the living room, yapping hysterically.

"I wonder who it could be this late," she murmured to herself, looking at kitchen clock. It was almost 9:30 pm.

Camille opened the door, grabbing Lila by the collar to keep her from running into the hallway.

"Oh, it's you," she said, smiling. "I didn't expect you until tomorrow. Come in!"

Her guest followed her into the apartment, smiling.

"I was getting all my stuff ready. I am so excited for this trip! I can't wait!" she gushed, turning her back for a moment.

She was about to turn again to offer a glass of wine, when she felt a sudden and exceptionally painful pressure against her throat.

"What are you doing?" she managed to whisper in a raspy and panicked voice, her fingers flying to her throat. She felt something there—thin, smooth, almost like Lila's braided nylon leash. As she fumbled with it, it tightened around her neck, and a warm breath grazed her cheek.

It occurred to her in a rush that she was being strangled. Why? Gasping for air, she tried to form the question, but the pressure on her throat was too much. All the dreams and wishes she'd had, all of her excitement for the future… they all seemed to be fading away, as her lungs began to ache. Hot tears dripped down her cheeks while her mascara melted into her eyes, making them burn.

The air was quickly leaving her lungs and her entire body started shaking from the fear of what was about to happen. She pounded futilely while her ballerina flats slipped on the floor as she tried to get her attacker to let go.

She desperately tried to gasp for air but it was impossible and her vision was growing blurry, a sharp pain spreading through her head.

Her dog's barking echoed through her ears and it felt like the loudest sound in the world, while the thudding of her heart began to slow.

She had never wished to be able to scream as much as she did in that moment.

But it wasn't possible.

The last thing she saw, before her vision faded, was Lila, whining at her feet, and then, absolute nothingness.

One

Phone at his ear, David Kenan paced his office, stopping every so often to look out the picture window, where the windshields from a river of cars stuck in afternoon traffic shone under the unrelenting California sun.

Fucking L.A., he thought, looking at the scene, wondering why he ever thought having a corner office that looked out onto that misery would be a good thing. *It may be hot, but some of the biggest snowflakes in the country are right here. And I'm lucky enough to have a blizzard of them as my clients.*

"Answer your goddamn phone, Tom," he barked to the sound of incessant ringing, raking a hand through his short blonde hair.

Finally, Tom Matthews answered the phone. "Good afternoon, Mr. Kenan," the man on the other end of the phone said, sounding far too calm and relaxed. "Did you make a decision on behalf of your client?"

"I did, Mr. Matthews, and I'd like to discuss the details we didn't go through the last time we spoke."

"Of course, of course. You name it, and it's done, Pal."

David sat at his wide desk, loosening the tie around his neck. It was so hot, he felt like he was about to melt, and all the pressure he'd been under the last few weeks hadn't helped. *Goddamn Wyatt. Biggest snowflake of them all.*

He took a deep breath, and not for the first time wondered why he'd gotten into this line of work in the first place. With his Harvard

Law degree, he could've been anyone. There was money in corporate law. Most of the top of the class went into that. But no, he'd thought entertainment law was more his thing. He'd had to move across country, schmooze with celebrities, make a name for himself among the Hollywood elite. He'd known some were prima donnas, but little did he know how bad it'd be. "First of all, as I mentioned before, I need to know that my client will be able to count on your absolute discretion."

"You got it, Davy, my boy. You don' worry about a thing, ol' Tom'll take care of that," Tom drawled in his deep southern accent.

They went on discussing the price to rent Firefly Cabin in a small community called Long Lakes. It was actually David's client, Wyatt, who had found the place, somewhere in the sticks of mid Tennessee. God only knew why he'd want to hide out in a place like that.

Actually, David knew. Wyatt had come from Nashville, believe it or not, in a different lifetime. But somewhere along the line, the boy had gone completely Hollywood and lost his mind. He'd become the snowflake to end all snowflakes, and now he was riding David's ass, trying to get him to seal the deal.

Apparently, he was hot to find a place where he could effectively hide for a while, and it was David's job, as his agent, to take care of everything else and do it quickly.

To tell you the truth, David thought, looking out on that midday traffic, *I wouldn't mind escaping out into the middle of the sticks right now, myself.*

"So, you'll have the place ready by tomorrow, correct?" David asked.

"I will, Bud. You got it, Davy."

"Perfect. I'll let my client know. Once again, please remember that you signed a confidentiality agreement, and that—"

"Yes, yes. Understood," Tom reassured him.

"All right," he mumbled. He trusted Tom, since his firm had arranged a couple of film shooting locations in mid Tennessee with

Tom's real estate business, but if Wyatt's location was disclosed to the press, there'd be hell to pay.

David hung up and glanced at his laptop, at the house he'd just rented for Wyatt.

Not much pleased his client, but this one ticked all the boxes. It was a huge, two-story log home that occupied four lakefront lots. It had a big yard and a three-car garage with a guest apartment on top, and the back sported a small deck and patio, furnished with long tables and benches, overlooking Firefly Lake. With three bedrooms, two bathrooms, a large, fully equipped kitchen, and a living room with a state-of-the-art entertainment system, there was plenty of room to spread out. It even had a basement complete with weight-lifting and cardio equipment, so he could keep up his training routine.

All that state-of-the-art luxury, buried right in the middle of absolutely nowhere.

There, Wyatt would be able to hide in peace; especially since Tom guaranteed him that nobody would disturb him during his stay there. *People around there like to keep to themselves,* Tom had promised. *They ain't those nosy folk who like to peek in windows and be in everybody's business. They won't come near him.* And, even if they did, who would recognize him in a place like that, all the way out in Nowheresville?

David smiled, satisfied, as he called Wyatt.

"Pack your bags. I'm buying you a plane ticket to Nashville for tonight as we speak," he said before his client even said Hello. Not that he ever said Hello. He usually started every conversation with, "Talk to me." *Typical Hollywood asshole.*

"Not tonight." Wyatt sounded a little drunk. Probably was. The guy never passed a bar he didn't like. *Just like most of my snowflake clients.*

But Wyatt wasn't just a snowflake, like most of his clients.

No, like it or not, David got to know his clients better than most therapists did. And he was afraid that Wyatt was more than just a drunk, and a fruitcake.

After what he'd seen, he had a very good reason to believe that Wyatt was a criminal.

Of course, David knew Wyatt would find something to complain about—the man always complained. All of his clients did. But David was used to his tantrums. *I don't know why I went to Harvard Law in order to be a glorified preschool teacher,* he'd complained to his wife, almost every evening.

"You told me you need to get out of here, fast. We got lucky, Wyatt," he reminded him. "This place is perfect. And you'd better be on this flight tonight if you know what's good for you."

"I… I… shit," Wyatt slurred. Definitely drunk. "I don't… get me on a flight tomorrow."

"Listen to me," David said, scrolling through the website for the airline and buying the ticket. "I have you on the red-eye leaving at midnight tonight. I'll get a car to take you to the airport. It'll be waiting for you. Got it?"

"Whatever," he barked before hanging up.

David rolled his eyes and tossed his phone on his desk.

Maybe some time in the countryside will help him with that horrible temper of his.

He'd done all he could. Now he could only hope that Wyatt would be able to keep calm and behave in those woods until it was time to come back home.

Two

I know I have anger management issues. The shrink keeps telling me that, insists that I should enroll in a program. Well, I'm not going to enroll in no damn program. I didn't even want to go to my shrink. I like my anger, it's my friend, it helps me carry on in this awful business. The people are all like sharks—they don't respect you unless you show them who's boss.

And when my anger gets the best of me, when my face—usually so easy to look at and serene—twists into that threatening grimace, watch out. People should know better than to annoy me—it never ends well for them. They lose all their self-importance and cower with their tail between their legs; it's easier to let me have it my way.

Of course, sometimes it's too late. Sometimes, my anger gets so strong that it completely numbs my brain, and that's when bad things start to happen. Really bad things. It's like I'm not me anymore. Somebody else is controlling my body. Somebody very mean.

But I'm starting to like that somebody, because I know they're protecting me from the others who want to control my life and take away what belongs to me. So I am embracing that person I become when anger blurs my judgement and everything is shrouded in a red cloud inside my head.

I like to call that person my very own 'guardian demon'.

Three

As Valentina stopped to massage her tired muscles from all the rowing she'd been doing around Firefly Lake, she took in the glass-calm waters, the warmth of the early October sun on her tanned Mediterranean skin, and the silence, interrupted only by the songs of birds among the trees and the cicadas chirping on the shore.

A shame that Jack can't be here, enjoying the peace with me.

She had to admit, she liked Long Lakes a lot better when it was like this, instead of how it'd been a couple months ago. That had been more excitement than she could handle. The whole business with the drug ring run by the Long Lakes' developer and spearheaded by the HOA president still had the neighborhood buzzing. Every time she thought about it, Valentina still couldn't believe that something like that actually happened. They'd almost been murdered themselves before the criminals were apprehended.

She had become very close to FBI Agent Jack Erikson, who she'd met while he was investigating a fraud case in the development over the summer. When that fraud case wound up being something far more sinister, he'd saved her life. Unfortunately, he'd gotten shot in the process, and required a lengthy hospital stay. Afterwards, he'd decided to spend his month-long medical leave with her at her cabin *Elsewhere*, making their relationship stronger and stronger every day. But once the wound was completely healed, he'd gone back to work at the field office in Memphis, three hundred miles west of Long Lakes, and now had his nose to the grindstone.

She guessed that kind of bravery went with the territory of being an FBI agent. Valentina, on the other hand, still shuddered every time she thought about it.

Long Lakes was a wonderful place in eastern Tennessee, a few miles from Cookeville. When she'd moved here a few years ago with her husband, Antonio, she'd thought they'd found their forever home in this idyllic, rural corner of the world. But he'd quickly lost interest, and eventually she'd learned there was another woman back home. They divorced soon after, and Valentina had stayed behind with her daughter, who was now a sophomore at the University of Tennessee. Valentina never had tired of the place, and enjoyed all of the amenities the gated community had to offer. Jack, too, had found himself right at home there.

It was strange to not have Jack around as much anymore, and kind of sad. She'd loved the time she spent with him—cooking for him, riding horses, going for slow walks in the woods together or simply listening to him playing the guitar. She realized how much she actually missed him every time she woke up in bed alone. She had gotten so used to his presence that now, when he wasn't there, the house felt emptier. Even Dante and Luna, her two lab mixes, seemed to miss him.

But she kept herself busy with her wine importing business, long hikes or horseback rides with Sunny and with her new favorite sport, kayaking, now that the weather was getting cooler and more bearable.

Also, she still had her hands full with cooking classic Italian recipes for her friend, Michelle, who lived just down the way.

Valentina checked her watch. Almost lunchtime. The thought of Michelle made her turn the kayak toward home. She and Michelle had agreed to meet at one; her friend was cooking a delicious chicken pot pie, and she didn't want to be late.

As soon as she tied the kayak to the wooden dock, she rushed inside, and immediately Luna and Dante ran to her, madly wagging their tails. She quickly patted them both before getting into the shower and, once she finished drying her thick mane of unruly black curls, took her bike and headed to Michelle's home.

Her friend was a waiting for her at the door, and as soon as she saw her, started to walk toward her, arms already open to give her a hug.

There were other people that Valentina liked in the community, but Michelle was her absolute best friend there. Their love for food was what had first brought them together after Valentina moved into the community and, from that point on, they'd continued exchanging delicious recipes at least once a week. At sixty-something years old, Michelle's culinary skills showed on her figure, giving her generous padding at the waist, whereas Valentina had managed to keep fit thanks to her love for the outdoors; horseback riding, kayaking, hiking and walking her dogs allowed her to keep her athletic figure even well in her forties.

Valentina smiled at her friend and showed her the bottle of Grignolino d'Asti she'd brought for lunch.

"This will certainly be the best wine for your amazing pot pie," Valentina explained, handing the wine to her friend. "I picked it especially because I thought it would pair well."

"I'd better open it and let it breathe right away then. Lunch is almost ready. Just a couple of minutes!"

Valentina followed Michelle inside her friend's cabin, which was a smaller but no less charming version of *Elsewhere*. The two sat at the table to chat while the food finished cooking.

"So how are things going? Is that a new tablecloth?"

Michelle nodded, beaming at the leaf-printed oilcloth over the table. "Oh, yes. I bought it from a catalog. I felt like it spiced things up a little for fall. What do you think?"

"It's very nice. Goes well with your rustic décor."

The smell of chicken was so heavenly, Valentina's stomach grumbled as Michelle opened the bottle and poured the wine. "But enough about that. Did you hear the news?" Michelle said, a spark in her eyes.

"What news?"

Valentina was never one for gossip, but hanging out with Michelle—who somehow always seemed to know everything about everyone—it was simply impossible not to be brought up to speed about everything that was going on in the community. She was second only to Lola—the community's star busybody.

"It seems that an actor has rented that huge house opposite you on the lake, Firefly Cabin!"

Valentina raised an eyebrow, trying to remember which cabin she was talking about. Oh, of course, she saw it every morning, mostly hidden by trees. It was that grand cabin that had been mostly empty ever since she'd moved in. "An actor—*here*?"

"I know, I know, at first I was skeptical myself. I figured it was just another nonsensical rumor started by Ellie or Lola. You know how they like to spice things up, keep things interesting. But the last time I saw her in the general store, Ellie swore up and down that she recognized him from some romantic comedy she'd been binging on Netflix."

"And who is this actor?"

"I think his name is Wyatt Rogers… Or something like that. Isn't that incredible?"

Valentina shrugged. The name didn't ring a bell, but she wasn't one for Hollywood, not like her daughter Bea, who seemed to follow all of their social media accounts, and knew just what each of them ate for breakfast.

The 'ding' of Michelle's oven interrupted the conversation and she got up to get the pie out.

"Anyway," Michelle went on, starting to plate the food, "I wonder what he's doing out here. He's probably not here to rub elbows with other movie stars, that's for sure."

"Definitely not! Maybe he just needed some peace and quiet."

"Most likely, yes." She shrugged. "Though it does make this place seem a lot more glamorous, don't you think?"

Valentina laughed. "Lola would disagree with you. She thinks she gives this place all the glamour it needs!"

They both laughed as they dug into the food. Valentina picked up a forkful of the wonderful smelling chicken in a thick broth, blew on it to cool it slightly, and took a taste. It was simply perfect. She closed her eyes, enjoying every single bite of her friend's amazing food.

"You were right," Michelle said, taking a sip of the wine. "This wine is perfect!"

Valentina smiled, satisfied with herself; when she moved to America from Italy, she'd started a wine importing business, and even though it was foreign territory at first, she was now practically an expert.

She took a sip herself, and had to agree. Good wine brought out the flavors in good food, making an ordinary meal into a taste experience. "I'm glad you think so."

Michelle poured more wine in both their glasses and, as they finished what was left of the pie, Valentina asked Michelle about her son, who was trying to fight his meth addiction; one of the many victims of the Long Lakes drug ring.

"Rehab has been hard for Rob," she explained with a frown, "But he's being doing way better so I'm trying to be optimistic. He tells me he might be out by Christmas. I'd love to spend the holidays with him. But we'll see. Fingers crossed."

Valentina held her friend's hand in hers, trying to comfort her. "I'm sure that you're proud of him for his progress."

"I am. I'm actually going to visit him soon at the center in Nashville."

"Oh… Do you need me to take care of Mina while you're away?" Michelle's cat was notoriously unhappy with being left alone for more than a few hours.

"Thank you, Valentina. You're such a sweet friend. I knew you'd offer. But you already have your dogs, so I couldn't impose on you. Besides, I already have someone coming to take care of her."

Valentina's ears perked up. "Oh? Who is it?"

"She's actually supposed to come here soon. Her name is Taylor Miller and she's incredible. Mina loves her, and I know that she's also been taking care of other animals around here. Everybody has been saying amazing things about her."

"I didn't hear anything about her," Valentina said, though she wasn't surprised, considering how little she heard about the community's gossip. She got up to help Michelle put the dishes away.

"She's new. Young. Really pretty. I think she just graduated college. She's been renting a small place right outside the gates, trying to figure out her next move. You know? But she's super convenient. So if you decide to go visit Jack in Memphis for a couple of days, I'm sure she would love to take care of your dogs."

"Maybe. I'll have to think about it."

Valentina had to admit, it would be nice to visit Jack. She got to see him so little these days. He'd been so busy with his new case that some days they didn't even have that much time to talk on the phone. A few times he'd said he might come back for the weekend, but it'd fallen through. Too much work to do. But he'd never suggested her going there, and she was worried that if she brought it up, he'd tell her it wasn't a good idea.

"So, what does Bea think about Jack? She's met him, right?"

"Oh yes," Valentina replied, beaming. "She totally accepted him, even before she met him. Actually, she's the one who convinced me to date him in the first place. She's so relieved that I am finally not alone anymore that she just dropped a bombshell on me! She wants to move out of Nashville and transfer to a new college in Miami!"

Michelle almost choked on her wine. "What? Why? I thought she liked Nashville. And what about her boyfriend?"

Valentina waved her hands in her own Italian way of expressing disappointment. "She says that people in Tennessee are too different from what she was expecting, and that Nashville is too small. She says she's ready to live—quote—'in a real city,' whatever that means. Her boyfriend wants to go with her, but the poor thing is a country boy at heart, so I doubt he will enjoy Miami. He loves her to pieces, but I'm afraid this change will be the end of their romance."

Michelle tutted. "And how do you feel about her transferring to a school in Florida?"

Valentina shrugged. "What can I say? She's big enough to make her own decisions and her own mistakes. Forcing her to stay would have just made her hate Tennessee even more. I guess I'm lucky she didn't decide to move to Seattle. That would be quite a trip to visit her!"

Michelle nodded in agreement. "But she'll still come home, right? To visit you?"

Valentina shrugged. "Well… I hope."

The truth was, this summer had been disappointing. She'd stayed in America because she loved it, but also as a home base for Bea, when she wasn't at school. But busy with internships and working, Bea had only come home once during the whole long summer, and that was after the incident with the drug ring.

She couldn't deny it. Her nest felt empty. She missed her only child. Jack had made things better, but now, even he wasn't around as much as she'd hoped.

"What does that mean?" Michelle asked, studying her friend closer.

"I don't know. I mean, I think I need a new hobby or something. Something to keep me busy," she said with a shrug.

Michelle's eyes sparkled. "Oh, dear. Valentina. You're already a renaissance woman. Cooking, wine, kayaking, horses, hiking… are you sure you need *another* hobby?"

Valentina giggled, shrugging off the loneliness that threatened to put her in a bad mood. She was about to say something else when a knock at the door interrupted her.

Michelle looked at the front door. "Oh, Taylor!" she called. "Come on in! We were just talking about you."

As soon as her visitor entered, she kneeled down to pet Mina, who slowly walked to her to rub her head against her leg, already purring. Seeing her, Valentina could understand why everybody was crazy about her. She was a bit short, with long blonde hair that flowed like silk midway down her back, and a pair of big green eyes that seemed just as kind as her smile. She probably wasn't much older than Bea, and had that same effervescent youthfulness that drew people in.

Michelle presented her with great flourish. "Taylor, this is my friend Valentina.”

“Nice to meet you,” Valentina said, offering the girl a smile. “I’ve heard many good things about you!”

Taylor’s eyes lit up in amazement. “Valentina? That’s a lovely name. And your accent… Where are you from, if I may ask?”

“I’m from Italy. I moved here about three years ago.”

“That’s amazing! I’ve always wanted to visit Italy. What part?”

“Milan.”

“Oh. You’ll have to tell me everything about it. Maybe one day I’ll be able to visit there, if my finances, and my schedule, permit. But right now, I’m in between careers, just trying to decide what to do with my life.”

Valentina couldn’t help but smile. “I’d love to.”

Michelle tapped her chin. “You know, Taylor, since you’re eager to make money, Valentina has two beautiful Labradors and she might need you soon.”

Taylor grinned. “Oh, that’s awesome! I’ll gladly take care of them. I love animals so much,” she gushed, gently lifting Mina into her arms and cuddling her.

Valentina nodded. “Well, I’ll let you know if I’ll need you.” *If Jack and I ever arrange for some time away.*

“Sure thing. Here.” She put Mina down to fish a small business card out of her pocket. “All my contact information is there.”

“Thank you very much. I’m afraid I have to dash now, guys, it’s getting late.”

Valentina put the business card in the pocket of her shorts and excused herself. As much as she would have loved to stay, the work was piling up for her wine business, and she’d planned to spend most of the afternoon on paperwork, the thing she liked least about the business.

On her way home, she texted Jack. *Hi! How are things in Memphis?*

A moment later, he came back with: *Busy as usual with the same old stuff. What’s new with you?*

She saw an opening there. She could hint about the possibility of spending time away, and maybe he would come up with the idea on his own. *Oh, lunch at Michelle's. Guess what? There's a new pet sitter in town. So I don't have to worry about what to do with Dante or Luna, if I ever decide to go away. Isn't that great?*

She stared at the phone, waiting with bated breath for his answer, so absorbed by it that she nearly tripped into a ditch on the side of the road. She caught herself just as his response came in: *Yeah. But when will you ever be able to take time away from the wine business?*

She sighed. Sometimes, he did not make things easy. She typed in: *Oh, I could, if something came along...*

Hint dropped. He'd have to be an idiot, not to read between the lines.

But she let out a grunt of disappointment when he responded with, *Well, who knows?*

By then, she'd reached her door, and had no appetite to finish her paperwork. All she could think about was a little holiday in Memphis. It really would have been a pleasant break from all the work that she'd been dealing with. She'd been so stressed lately.

Once she was home again, though, she didn't have the time to sit at her desk. Her phone rang with a call from her daughter, Bea.

"Ciao, tesoro!"

"Hey, Mom! I was calling to see how you were doing."

Valentina smiled; since that horrible experience, Beatrice called even more often than usual, always making sure her mother was okay and that she wasn't going to have a mental breakdown.

Bea, like her father, worried way too much. Everything considered, she was perfectly fine, just a bit shaken at the memory of it, but that was it.

"I'm fine, Bea, don't worry," she said, opening her laptop.

In front of her, through the window of her studio, she could see the calm waters of Firefly Lake, so blue that it looked like a fresh painting. She leaned over and opened the window to let the fragrance of the surrounding woods in, taking a deep gulp of the fresh air.

"Tell me about you," she said to her daughter. "How are

classes?”

“Ugh… Miami is looking better and better.”

Valentina laughed. Beatrice did not like to speak about her classes, but what college student did? “Don’t tell me you’re failing anything?”

“No. No. I’m doing okay, Mom, still fighting with that Persuasive Writing class.”

“I know—that teacher and you sure don’t get along!” She shook her head, her lips spread in a smile that disappeared the moment her daughter changed the subject to mention Antonio, her now-remarried, insufferable ex-husband.

“Dad’s worried about you. I know you don’t really want to talk to him, but after what happened to you—”

“You’re right,” she interrupted her. “I do *not* want to talk to your father, and even though I appreciate his concern, you can tell him that I don’t need it.”

After Antonio married Manuela, the woman that he’d cheated on her with, their already thin communication became even thinner and, after Valentina met Jack, she officially didn’t want to have anything to do with her ex-husband unless it involved Bea.

She had to admit it: not talking with Antonio was *amazing,* and Valentina was determined to keep it that way.

Her daughter sighed on the other end of the line, but clearly she knew Valentina was too stubborn to have her mind changed. Smartly, she dropped the matter.

“Hey, guess what?” Valentina asked mostly so that they wouldn’t have to talk about Antonio anymore.

“What?”

“Apparently there is an actor renting Firefly Cabin.”

“Are you kidding?! What actor? Please tell me it’s Chris Hemsworth!”

“I wish, but no, nobody that famous. His name is Wyatt Rogers, I think.”

“Uhm… I’ve never heard of him. But still, it’s kind of cool.

Have you met him?"

"Not yet. Apparently, he acts in some kind of romantic comedy on Netflix."

"Well, when you do meet him, let me know if he's hot. And young. And single. And interested in Italian girls."

Valentina rolled her eyes. "I have to go now, *tesoro*, I've got a lot of work to do."

"Okay, Mom. I love you. Say 'hi' to Jack for me."

"I will, and I love you too."

After she hung up, she started working, but she kept getting distracted, thinking about her possible weekend with Jack. She'd have to keep working on him, dropping casual hints, and maybe he'd get the picture, eventually.

As she worked, she realized she hadn't told Jack about the rumor. But if there was anyone who cared less about movie stars, it was Jack Erikson. He didn't even really like movies all that much. Mostly, for entertainment, he listened to classical music and read big history tomes, or played his guitar.

But in Long Lakes it was easy not to care about Hollywood. It was practically a world away.

Not anymore, apparently.

And she had the feeling even Jack would find the news of Long Lakes' newest resident kind of thrilling.

Four

The alarm clock went off while Jack was in the midst of a dream. It was a pleasant one, but the second the blaring sound suddenly erupted throughout the hotel room, loud and annoying, it slipped away, and he couldn't grasp what it was about.

He rolled onto his side, rubbing his eyes, lying there for a second, just letting the damn alarm clock scream on the nightstand.

Valentina. It had been about Valentina.

Damned if he could remember anything else about it.

He finally stretched an arm out to turn it off and to check if Valentina had answered his text from last night.

She hadn't yet. In fact, none of the text messages he'd received were from her.

His message was still hanging out there, unanswered: *Have a good night.*

Struggling to a sitting position, he propped up his pillows against the cushioned headboard and let his head fall against it as he scanned through the rest of his work messages from various associates.

Work, work, work. It never ended. There was a time, not so long ago, when he'd had his FBI badge pinned on his chest, that he'd been so damn proud.

Now he had to wonder what it was all for. The fraud department was depressing. Damn depressing. Everyone was out to cheat someone.

Either that, or even worse. He'd learned that last summer, and still had the scar from the bullet wound in his shoulder to remind him of it.

And then there was Valentina…

He tried his best not to let the bad mood he'd been in lately because of his stressful job take charge and impinge on his home life. Valentina had become an important part of his life, and he didn't want to screw that up. Not the way he'd messed things up with his ex-wife, Yvonne, by being physically and emotionally unavailable, consumed by his job. So though his work had taken him away to Memphis, he made sure to check in with her often.

But sometimes he felt like Valentina was pulling away.

It was silly, though. He knew that Valentina had worked until very late the day before, so she'd probably just forgotten to answer him before falling asleep. No big deal, no reason to freak out or get irritated.

Then why was he so annoyed?

He was about to throw his phone to the side when he saw another email from his boss asking for—no, *demanding*—another update. That was Dees. Special Agent in Charge Bruce Dees, a late fifties, no-nonsense, never-smiling former military guy who still had the buzz cut to show for it. He stalked around the office, barking orders, and usually he got what he wanted, because most people were too scared to face his wrath.

Lately, though, Dees had been on his ass about the case more than usual. And, so far, Jack had no idea on how to close it. He had been assigned to investigate a huge company, Memphis Brokerage, Inc., suspected of fraud. The Stock Exchange Commission had contacted the FBI because they noticed that somebody bought a good amount of shares of a very important US stock right before a Saudi Arabian fund bought a three-percent share of that same stock. Whoever purchased those shares had made a fortune out of one single transaction. The timeline was suspicious to say the least, and screamed *insider trading* to Jack's sensitive ears.

Jack knew that the managing director, Bret Copland, would want to supervise such a big operation, therefore he was the person he was focusing on most, yet he hadn't been able to figure out how he had fooled the system. Everything about him, so far, seemed clean. Usually it just took one tiny misstep—one small thread, when pulled, would send the whole operation unravelling. He just needed to find it.

But he couldn't. Everywhere he looked… dead ends. And until he found it, he couldn't return home.

Not only that, but he had been trying to reach out to his kids since he left for Memphis but, as usual, Yvonne was refusing to let him have any type of contact with them. Last time he'd heard from or seen them was after that mess that went down at Long Lakes. It was ridiculous! They were his kids too, for God's sake. Yvonne seemed to be doing everything in her power to keep him from his kids, and yet she'd be the first one to call him a deadbeat.

With everything going on, Valentina not answering him definitely didn't help.

First things first, he told himself as he swung his legs over the side of the bed. *I'll look at the files again. There's got to be something I'm missing. Having fresh eyes will help.*

He could not afford to screw this up. Yes, he'd had success busting that drug circle at the community, but his boss never failed to remind him that drug busts weren't in his job description. *This* was.

He grabbed the phone again, tapping the screen while looking at the latest messages he exchanged with Valentina. He couldn't deny how much he missed her, especially right now. Way more that he was expecting, if he was completely honest with himself.

Even though he and Valentina had been dating for only a couple of months, she was becoming more and more important to him, to the point where it hurt to be away from her for that long. It was scary to think about how much he came to care about her considering how his marriage ended, but he couldn't deny his feelings.

However, she didn't seem as involved. That definitely worried him. She'd been hurt before. What if things went terribly wrong again? What if he was falling too hard while she was just trying to take things slow? What if he totally misunderstood everything from the beginning?

Are you seriously going to act like an insecure teenager? he asked himself, staring at the screen that had now turned black, and contemplating his reflection, showing the tired face of a forty-something with slanted blue-green eyes and disheveled black hair already showing some grey at the temples. He was probably just letting all the stress get the better of him. Yeah, that was exactly what it was.

He just needed to calm down and try to focus on cracking the case. The quicker he did that, the quicker he could see Valentina again and the easier it would be for him to not think about how much he missed his kids.

He sighed, answering his boss's email, letting him know that he would have him a complete report by the end of the week. Then he got up and stretched, and took a second to look at the view outside of his hotel's room. It was nothing special, just a side street in the city with a row of brick buildings, but it was relaxing to watch the morning sunlight caressing the very top of the roofs while a couple of clouds slowly moved through the sky.

Jack took a deep breath, trying to convince himself that everything was going to be okay, even though, once again, Valentina's absence pulled a string latched on to his heart, making it hurt.

He decided to try and relax with a nice, hot shower before getting back to work. He went to the bathroom and turned on the water, then climbed in. Letting the hot water fall on him, making his skin slowly turn red, he stared at the cracks on the wall's tiles, completely lost in his thoughts. If he wanted to get this case done and get Dees off his back, he really had to up his game. It was almost surreal to think that he was the one who destroyed an entire drug circle without any expertise, when he couldn't seem to be able to close a stupid fraud case, something he'd been training in for years.

As he was wrapping a towel around his waist, his phone started to ring. He rushed to it, hoping that it would be Valentina, or maybe one of his kids who'd been able to snatch the phone from their mother.

His heart jumped when he saw Valentina's face light up on the screen. He answered on the first ring, and sunk down onto his unmade bed. "Hey, you."

"Hey, Jack! So sorry I didn't answer your last text. I was exhausted."

He smiled, relieved to hear her voice, even if she sounded kind of tired. "Don't worry. I totally understand. I am not in the best shape myself, to be honest."

"Still having problems with the case?"

"Yeah… And you know all about Dees. He's a ballbreaker, and he's hot to get results. He won't stop nagging me about it!"

"I'm sorry about that, but I have faith in you. I'm sure you'll close it soon."

He smiled, putting her on speaker while he got into a pair of jeans and sniffed at a shirt that he dropped on a chair the night before, deciding that it was still wearable. He put it on and then sprayed a little bit of cologne on his neck, just to make sure. Meanwhile, Valentina told him about how beautiful it had been on the lake during yesterday's kayaking trip. "I didn't want to come in, but I had that lunch with Michelle. So I gave in. She made her pot pie."

"Ah, her legendary pot pie," he teased, though he felt a sad longing in his chest. He could've done with some down-home cooking. Valentina was the best of cooks.

After that, the conversation turned to what he'd been doing. He told her about his boring day yesterday, stuck under a pile of paper, as he grabbed his phone, and headed out of the hotel to the nearby Waffle House. He could have had breakfast at the motel, but after all that talk about down-home cooking, nothing was more depressing to him than starting the day with a sad complimentary hotel breakfast.

Even after he ordered and while he was eating, he stayed at the phone with Valentina, so glad to finally be able to talk to her. But as they went on, she seemed to get distracted. She started saying "Mmmhmm," to everything he said, and seemed rushed.

"Am I keeping you from something?" he finally asked her.

"Oh, no. Not really. Well… actually. I have a bunch of paperwork to catch up on for the business. I started doing it yesterday afternoon but I was so tired."

"I hope you're all right? Not getting a touch of the flu?"

Again, she said, "Mmmhmmm." Then, she seemed to realize what he was saying, because she said, "Oh, no. I'm perfectly fit. Never felt better. Just… guess I haven't been sleeping very well at night. You know."

He did. Valentina was a proud woman, and would never say she couldn't handle something herself. But she'd finally broken down before and admitted that it was hard to sleep alone, at night, after the terrible events they'd gone through during the summer. He assumed that was what she was hinting at.

At least, he hoped it was that, and not anything more serious.

For a moment, he had a flashback to Yvonne. Jack had gradually started spending more and more time at work, and that had thrown his first wife into the arms of another man. He pushed those thoughts away. Valentina was far less flighty, and the victim of a two-timing ex-spouse, also. She would never do such a thing.

Still, he couldn't help but wonder…

Once she hung up, he kept drinking his dark coffee, tracing the edge of the cup with his finger. He felt a bit better now that he'd had a chance to talk to her, but she still felt distant for some reason. Maybe something really was wrong. Maybe he should've asked her, point blank, to tell him if there was anything on her mind. Anything at all she wanted to get out. They were in a relationship, after all.

No. He didn't want to sound paranoid or too clingy but at the same time he also wanted to make sure that she was happy. Maybe she wasn't anymore, or maybe she was just too busy with work to keep the honeymoon phase going. He let out a long breath and tried to put it out of his mind; he'd never been very good at understanding women. The best thing he could do was finish this case so he could go back to Valentina and ask her in person. That would solve everything.

Once he was done with his coffee, he headed out toward Memphis Brokerage's main office. It was almost a one-hour walk from the Waffle House, but he really needed to get some fresh air. It'd do him good after spending so much time holed up in that hotel room, going through files for the better part of the week.

When Jack got to the large, modern building, that was all sleek black windows, a short woman with a blond bun and a pair of thick red glasses welcomed him with a smile that didn't quite seem genuine. He knew why; the last time that he was there, he'd had her fetch some documents from their archives that the FBI had deemed pretty suspicious.

Not that it had done much good. Despite receiving the requested documents that day and working all afternoon trying to connect the dots, he wasn't able to find anything useful and was forced to head out with his tail between his legs. The managing director, Bret Copland, a short, weaselley guy with a silver comb-over, had walked him to the tall glass door with a smug and awfully irritating grin on his face, like, *Better luck next time, Bozo.*

This time, though, Jack would be more meticulous, now that he knew who he was messing with. He was sure he'd find something. So when the secretary greeted him, he quickly showed the warrant he'd presented the last time and walked to the elevator with no intention of losing any time. He reached the manager's office and loudly knocked at the door. As he did, another secretary leapt up from behind her desk, a panicked look on her face, and nearly jumped in front of him, trying to bar his way.

"Sir! Mr. Copland is in a very important meeting. I'd be happy to make you an appointment…"

"I'm from the FBI," Jack barked back, quickly shoving his badge in front of her face. "It's important. I'm sure that Bret will understand if I have to interrupt his meeting."

Before the secretary could say anything else, the office door opened.

"What is going on here, Milly?"

The moment the man recognized Jack, he froze in the doorframe and muttered something that sounded like a curse under his breath. But he quickly got his composure back and gave him the same condescending smile he'd given him the last time, when he practically pushed him out of the building.

"Mr. Erikson. Here for another visit, I see. Can't get enough of us, can you?"

"No. In fact, I would love to take another look at some of your transactions. Not just for the date in question, but for the entire month before, and after, if you wouldn't mind."

"Are you sure?" Copland blurted out, his face turning red. When Jack looked at him in surprise, he said, "I'm just concerned, that's an awful lot of receipts. You're going to be buried in them."

Jack waved his hand in the air. "I don't mind. Just set me up in an open conference room and I'll be out of your hair shortly."

"But of course! Like I told you last time, we have nothing to hide. I run a very honest company."

"Yeah. I'm sure you do. But we still have i's to dot and t's to cross. I'm sure you understand, so just get me those files, Bret."

Copland scoffed. "Well, I'm afraid I'm in a meeting at the moment, but my assistant will be happy to show them to you."

Jack nodded and followed the still-confused woman toward her desk, where she let him access her computer, while Copland stared at Jack from his office doorway. Jack smiled at him. Copland retreated into his office and slammed the door.

Two hours later, in the brokerage's main conference room, surrounded by at least a dozen banker's boxes full of receipts, Jack was ready to pull his hair out. He scrubbed his hands down his face. He got up from the chair so abruptly that it slid against the wall behind the desk.

Nothing. He'd found absolutely nothing.

He quickly left the building, refusing to give Copland the satisfaction of kicking him out again, then meandered back to the hotel, feeling completely defeated. What would he say to Dees now? How would he justify that pompous prick making a fool of him for a second time?

As if the situation wasn't bad enough already, at that moment his phone buzzed with a call from his ex-wife. Cursing under his breath, he lifted it to his ear.

"Now is really not a good time," Jack barked.

"Of course! You're up my ass for weeks because you want to talk to the kids, but the moment I call you back, it's not a good time? Why am I not surprised, Jack?"

He pressed his fingers on the bridge of his nose, frustrated and irritated. This day just kept getting worse and worse. He let her keep blabbering on, while walking at a clipped pace back to the hotel, his head down and his mood even sourer.

"Do you even care about your children at all? Why do you keep calling me if you can't even find a bit of time for them, huh?" Yvonne continued, as he struggled to get the key to the hotel room out of his pocket. "Fine. It's your loss. I was going to suggest you take the kids for an outing next weekend, but maybe I should just forget it."

Shit. He'd blown it. That's all he'd ever wanted with his kids—some time to be with them, before they grew up and decided they didn't even know him anymore. He took a deep breath and forced his voice to be calm. "Yvonne, I'm sorry."

She let out a bitter laugh. "You're a real class act, Jack." There was a long pause. "So?"

"So, what? You expect me to respond to that?"

"No, I'm asking you. Next Saturday night. Do you want to take the kids overnight for some weekend bonding, or not?"

"Yeah, of—" He caught himself and exhaled, long and low. "Next Saturday… Hell, Yvonne. I told you. I need more notice than that, I—"

"I get it. You're too busy for your kids. As usual."

He sucked in a breath. Again, there she was, manipulating things the way she always did to her benefit. He couldn't believe she was the same woman he'd met and fallen in love with years earlier. "So what's the big event?"

"Huh?"

"You never ask me to watch them. So, what's going on? Weekend plans in the city? A location wedding? What?"

She let out a cry of frustration. "If you must know, my sister's getting married in Cape Cod. But that's neither here nor there. Your work always comes first."

"If you knew she was getting married, you should've told me earlier," he said. "I'm in Memphis on a case and I can't get away. Will you please let me speak to them?"

"No, I won't, Jack! And you know why? Because you constantly pretend like you care for my kids but you don't!"

She could always do that to him—no matter how hard he tried to keep calm, she knew just what to do to push his buttons. His composure shattered, he exploded. "*Your* kids? They're my kids too, in case you freakin' forgot!"

"Don't you dare use that tone with me!" she snarled. "Don't try to call again!"

He opened his mouth to say something, but realized he was speaking to dead air. She'd hung up.

Jack threw the phone on the bed before slumping to the floor, tears in his eyes. Hell. Why had he said that to her? He missed his kids so much. He would have given anything to speak with them but when it came to Yvonne, she knew just how to use their kids as a weapon against him.

He looked down at his shoes. He needed to let Dees know that his latest visit to Memphis Brokerage had been a massive disappointment. But not right now.

Now, he just wanted to get a six-pack, hole up in his bleak hotel room, and wallow in his misery—alone.

Five

Wyatt Rogers looked around the large living room of Firefly Cabin for the hundredth time and let out an exasperated sigh. Raking his hands through his longish hair, he paced around the couch, the wooden floor creaking under his feet.

Intolerable. This is intolerable. Back in L.A., I'd be out at a club, six different beautiful women competing for my attention.

Now the only thing he had competing for his attention were the mosquitoes. He'd forgotten how bloodthirsty they were in this corner of the world, and, of course, he hadn't even thought of packing bug spray. The mosquitoes had eaten him alive last night while he tried to relax on the hammock on the back porch, under the stars.

But it wasn't just that. It was everything. The place was gorgeous, a blast from his childhood, but he'd long since outgrown that. And there was nothing but trees, trees, nature, and more trees. And mosquitoes. Snore. He had only been there for a week and was already completely bored out of his mind. That morning he'd even called David to at least have someone to chat with. But, of course, David was busy as usual and told him to hang in there.

He had scoffed. Easy for him to say. He wasn't the one stuck in that muddy hellhole.

Now he remembered why he was so eager to leave Tennessee when he was younger. Nothing happened in this damn place. Even if that was the whole point of this trip—giving him a chance to lie low and relax—he now had to admit it to himself. He was going crazy.

The only interesting thing that had happened to him so far was seeing that cute woman kayaking on the lake out back, but he still had no idea who she was or how to make contact with her.

Besides, David told him to keep a low profile and to do his best not to interact with anybody. But now, Wyatt was craving even the smallest event or interaction.

As he walked toward the fridge to get a beer, he realized how much he missed L.A.

He sat down on the couch and turned on the television, thinking about all the lavish parties, all the beautiful clubs that were the staple of his exciting life. His eyes darted toward the window where there was nothing but trees. Then he looked at the television where he'd found all he could get were three channels. One had fly-fishing 24/7.

Fly-fishing. As if he wanted to think of his dad. His abusive dad, who actually used to throw lit cigarettes at him, hoping they'd set him on fire.

And he'd come back here… why, again?

"This is ridiculous!" he said, slamming the beer on the coffee table so that a little bit of it frothed out.

He threaded his hands in his hair and decided to drive to that one Piggly Wiggly that he'd passed when he got to the community. Luckily he had a rental car, which meant he could probably take a few drives. That is, if there was anyplace good to drive to. The Piggly Wiggly was prime entertainment for this armpit of the world. His fridge was almost completely full thanks to the service David had hired to supply him with the necessities, but any excuse to get out was a good one.

Wyatt quickly put on his shoes, a baseball cap, sunglasses and a simple hoodie. It horrified him to be seen in public that way, but he knew that if he dressed too fancy he might attract attention and blow his cover. This ensemble actually qualified him as high society in this corner of Tennessee, where most people were considered upper crust as long as they didn't have meth mouth.

He drove fast through the community, dust flying all around the Mercedes C Class that he had David rent for him. His agent had wanted to put him in some old piece of crap Camry, to keep the prying eyes off him. But Wyatt had drawn a line; when it came to cars, he refused to get into anything that didn't look comfortable and drive with a little style.

He drove through the small town of Pikeville, observing the beaten-down mobile homes, the sad, old stores on the cracked, dirty sidewalks, and the few people walking around, most wearing Walmart duds like cheap T-shirts and ill-fitting jeans that were in fashion… oh, just about *never*. Most of the women had perms and the men mullets, as if they hadn't realized the eighties had ended. It was a completely different world from what he was used to.

He finally arrived at the grocery store, the high, hot sun reflecting on his dark sunglasses as he parked in the crowded lot. Apparently no one around here worked a normal nine-to-five job. He got out of his car and walked through the busy parking lot, taking in the local flavor with a bit of amusement. A bunch of cub scouts, collecting coins at the front of the store. A homeless man, playing a harmonica. A couple of young whores in belly-shirts, skipping school, who'd probably be pregnant by the time they were fifteen.

Ah, rural Tennessee.

He'd gotten better than this. Gone to Hollywood the day he graduated and never looked back. Scored a couple of commercials, then a few television sit-coms, and then he hit the big time with Netflix. It was only a matter of time before major motion picture studios came calling. He could feel it.

But he'd already shattered the expectations of anyone in this hellhole. Years ago, his high school outside of Nashville had named him Person of the Year, and when they called him to ask him if he'd come by to accept, he'd told them "No way in hell." He'd moved on to bigger and better, where the people actually mattered. Where he could hang out with other important people. People like him were made to be *served* by people like this. He didn't remember the last time he'd done his own grocery shopping. The moment he could afford it, he'd hired a lady to do it for him. It was simply too tedious a task, a waste of time.

But hell. As bored as he was, he figured he might as well give it a shot.

He walked aisle after aisle, unimpressed by all the offerings as his eyes darted from shelf to shelf. Every so often he would take a look at the other clients walking around, disgusted by the amount of overweight people that he kept seeing. His body was his temple and he could never understand how people could let themselves get to the point where they could barely walk.

With a grimace of disgust he kept going, taking longer than necessary and walking as slowly as possible, so desperate was he for a distraction. He could almost hear David's voice in his head, telling him not to go out unless it was absolutely necessary.

He picked up the bug spray he desperately needed as well as a few random unessential items and, as he walked to the counter, shook his head. These people were so dumb they probably shared the same brain cell. David had always been paranoid.

As he waited on the line, checking the headlines on *People* and *Entertainment Weekly* to see if there was anything about him, and wishing they would get with the program and put in a self-checkout, he noticed a pretty woman staring at him from one of the other lines. With her trim figure and blonde hair, she definitely stood out among this sea of whales. She had a confused wrinkle on her forehead, and her gaze was intent on him.

Wait… did she actually recognize him?

Hmm, maybe I could…

No. No, that wouldn't be a good idea. David's words in his head, he looked away. This might be bad. He only hoped she wouldn't make a scene. He screwed his hat lower over his brow, trying to ignore her.

The next time he glanced back, the woman had a huge cheek-to-cheek smile even as she advanced to the register and began placing her groceries on the conveyor belt.

Great. Once she's done paying, she's probably going to wait for me, he thought to himself. *And then she's going to make a scene.*

By the time it was Wyatt's turn to pay, though, he couldn't spot her anywhere. He sighed in relief, although he was kind of hoping that the woman would have waited for him. She was beautiful, after all. Screw David. It could've been nice to talk with someone, maybe even get her to help him pass the time…

No. Probably better if you don't. You know what happens when you play with fire.

As he approached his car in the lot, he realized the woman was parked next to him, loading groceries into the trunk of her Honda Civic. She smiled broadly when she noticed him.

"Can I help you?" he said, opening the trunk of his car.

The woman blushed a bit. "Yes, well, I thought I recognized you from one of my favorite TV shows. But then I thought I must be crazy. A movie star? In Pikeville?"

Her laugh was infectious. He laughed back. "Maybe it's not *so* crazy."

Her jaw dropped. "So it *is* you?"

"In the flesh."

Her laugh became a girlish giggle, and she tucked her short blond hair behind her ear. He realized that she was even more beautiful that he initially thought. She was petite, with nice, toned legs that were visible from under her white skirt. Her straight, shiny hair reached her shoulders, her eyes were big and dark, her nose small and her lips full. Also, she was very skinny, which was a great plus for him.

"I figured this might have been your car," she went on, gazing at it. "Seems pretty fancy."

Wyatt smiled, slamming the trunk shut as she offered him her hand.

"I'm Melissa."

He shook her hand, noticing how soft her skin was. "Well, I guess I don't really need to introduce myself, do I?"

She chuckled, getting her phone out of her purse. "Could I maybe bother you for a picture, Mr. Rogers?"

"Oh, please, you can call me Wyatt."

She blushed even more and got closer to him, took the picture and looked at it like it was the most precious thing she possessed in the whole world.

"Thank you so much! I can't believe this is really happening. I mean, an actor here, in this forgotten land?"

He laughed. "Yeah, I just needed some peace and quiet. Work has been stressful recently."

"I can't even imagine." She started to look around, clearly not wanting to let him go.

At that moment, Wyatt didn't want to go, either. This meeting was perfect; she was a beautiful woman and it seemed like she'd been placed here, just for him. He wouldn't have minded getting to know her better, spending some more time with her, especially considering how much he was missing human interaction.

"I'd love to stay, Melissa, but unfortunately I can't let anybody else recognize me," he explained, gazing furtively around the lot. "Or my plan to get some peace would be ruined."

"I understand." She bit on her lip in an irresistible way.

For a moment, he imagined holding the woman in his arms, stripping her bare, touching and holding her, and he nearly groaned aloud. *Fucking David.* "It was very nice to meet you, though. I wish I could take you out to dinner somewhere, but—"

He opened the door to his car and was surprised when she placed a hand on it, stopping him in his tracks. Her eyes gleamed with hidden meaning. "We could have dinner at my place. I live alone. Nobody would bother us there."

Wyatt smiled and turned back toward her. "Now that's an idea. Where do you live?"

She named the place, but he shrugged. "Never heard of it. I don't know too many places around here."

"Where do you live?"

"Uh… Long Lakes."

"Oh, wow. My place is in another gated community, not too far from you. I can give you directions, and you can meet me there later tonight?"

"That's perfect," he said. *Yes! Screw David. What he doesn't know won't hurt him.* "Thank you for the invitation. I'd love to have dinner at your place!"

Melissa grinned. "We could go right now, if you'd like. I usually eat around this time, anyway."

Wyatt checked his watch. It was almost six. "Works for me," he said. "I'll follow your car."

As Wyatt drove around the winding roads through the countryside and the woods, following Melissa, he thought about how lucky he was. Well, David might not think so, but David was all the way in L.A., and Wyatt was here. About to get laid by what was probably one of the few beautiful, alluring women in this part of the state.

Yes, he could feel it. This was his lucky night.

Finally, Melissa's small red car turned onto a narrow road and, not too long after that, they were in front of her house. It was white wood-shingled, with a porch and a fenced postage-stamp-sized yard with a swing set.

"You have kids?" Wyatt asked, when he joined her on the curb.

"Oh, no, that's for my niece. She and my sister come visit so often that I just thought it would be nice for her to have something to entertain herself with. I live alone. Well, with Cupcake."

"Cupcake?"

"My dog!"

"I see. What brings you out here… with Cupcake?" he motioned to the groceries. "Here, let me help with that."

He grabbed some of her groceries and she thanked him. "Oh, you know. Most of my family is in Knoxville. But what can I say? I moved out here because I was chasing a boyfriend. The relationship didn't last. But my love affair with the outdoors did. I like it more rural, and I love hiking. So this is the best place for it."

He heard the Pomeranian yipping even before she opened the door.

Great. A dog.

She leaned down and petted the dog as she stepped in. He resisted the urge to kick it and smiled. He lowered a hand to pet it. "Nice dog…"

It snapped at him. He snatched his hand away.

Melissa giggled. "Oh, that's Cupcake. He only really likes me." She gave the animal a frown and talked in that annoying baby-talk pet owners seemed to reserve for their pets. "Don't you, Mr. Cupcake?"

He turned away, significantly less interested in Melissa, now. The house was cozy and organized. It reminded him of the house he used to live in with his family, back before he moved to L.A.

"Just sit down and relax," Melissa said, pointing at the couch as she put her groceries on the kitchen counter.

Yip yip!

"What's gotten into you, Cuppy?" She glowered at the dog as he sat down. "Can I offer you anything to drink? I've got some Prosecco. It's probably not as good as what you are used to, but it will be better than nothing."

Yip yip!

"Wine would be awesome. Thank you."

"And what would you like to eat? I have to admit, I was not expecting something so amazing to happen to me today. I'm… I'm unprepared."

Yip yip! She grabbed the dog by his collar and blushed.

He shrugged. "I don't want to be any trouble. Whatever you've got will be perfectly fine."

Yip yip!

She frowned at the dog as she opened the wine bottle. "Okay. Any more noise out of you and you're going in the garage!"

The dog squealed, reprimanded.

Melissa gave Wyatt a glass of wine and tried to relax. But the dog jumped on the couch, next to him, and began to slobber on him. He tried to shove him away.

"All right! That's it." She shook her head and led the dog away by the collar. "I'm sorry, Wyatt."

"No trouble." *Thank God.*

She removed the dog from the area, then took pots and pans out of the cabinets and set to cooking a simple meal of chicken and vegetables.

Luckily, once she locked the Pomeranian in another room, things improved. She put on music, and it drowned out his annoying barks. Wyatt offered to help and together they drank wine and cooked while she peppered him with questions about his life in L.A. and the series he was working on.

The food was delicious. The company even better. Afterwards, they watched a movie together on the sofa, laughing and relaxing as if they were two old friends.

Things were going so well that he decided to make a move on her. He put his hand on her leg, caressing it gently. He could feel her tense but she didn't stop him, so he scooted a bit closer to her.

Her body stiffened even more. "This movie is hysterical," she said, probably to break the tension that she was feeling.

"It is! It was a great choice, like it was a great choice for me to spend some time with you. You're such an amazing woman."

"You really think so?" she whispered, her face reddening as he tucked some of her hair behind her small ear to see her face better.

"I do," he said as he gazed into her eyes. "And I don't often meet women that impress me, I can assure you."

She laughed. "Now you're just being nice. God knows how many gorgeous women you meet every day. I'm no comparison."

She looked down and he put a hand under her chin to make her look back up at him.

"I'm serious. Yeah, a lot of those women seem beautiful but most of them are just fake and incapable of having a conversation. You're a real woman and I really like that; I wish I could meet more women like you."

"I'm flattered, Wyatt."

He smiled. "It's only the truth."

Their eyes locked for a second and he slowly leaned in to kiss her. Her lips were soft and tasted slightly like the wine that they had been drinking.

He could feel her smiling against his lips as he put his hands around her tiny waist. They kissed until they had to stop to catch their breath. She grabbed his hand to lead him toward her bedroom, where she lay back on the mattress, waiting for him to explore the rest of her.

He did, and enjoyed every last moment of it. From her responses, so did she.

Afterwards he lay on the mattress, breathing heavily, a small drop of sweat rolling down the side of his temple. He watched the fan rotating slowly on the ceiling, offering them a bit of relief from the heat of the room, while Melissa curled by his side, the sheets tangled between her legs.

"That was incredible," she said, still catching her breath.

Wyatt looked at her, satisfied. "I have my moments," he joked.

"Oh, clearly, you do."

They both laughed and cuddled for a little more. "Hey," she said, tickling his side and jumping out of the bed. "I think I want to take a shower. Join me?"

He didn't have to be asked twice. He followed her into the bathroom, already looking forward to round two. She turned on the water, letting the steam slowly waft through the air, casting everything in a dream-like state. He didn't even mind that her place was a dump. He didn't mind that the shower was downright claustrophobic, barely big enough for one person. He'd use that to his advantage tonight.

Wyatt let the cool water fall on his sweaty skin while admiring Melissa's figure in front of him. He hugged her, kissed her neck, making her giggle, and then helped her soap herself.

They stayed in there until they were prunes, and made love again, against the shower wall. When they were clean, he stepped out, wrapping a towel around his waist, and checked the time on the bedside clock. It was almost eleven.

"You could spend the night if you'd like," Melissa offered, resting her head on his shoulder so that her hair lightly tickled his bare skin.

"I'd love to, but I have some things to take care of with my agent. I was actually supposed to call him. I'd better get going."

He'd used that line with plenty of women, but this time it was the truth. This time, though, he would've loved to stay. It sure beat the bleak, empty house waiting for him at Firefly Lake.

"Oh… Okay…" She seemed disappointed but didn't say anything as he dressed. When he was done, she was still silent as she walked him to the door.

"I had a lovely time, Melissa. Thank you so much for your hospitality."

He cupped her face and kissed her forehead gently.

"Thank you! I still can't believe that I just slept with my favorite actor," she gushed. "Maybe we can do this again sometime?"

"I'm counting on it. But remember, though, you can't tell anybody about this."

She nodded. "I promise."

He kissed her hand and started to walk toward his car. The air was cooler now and a couple of stars were visible through the tall trees.

"You can call me anytime," she said from the porch, her hair wet and sexy, veiling one eye.

"I will," he responded, waving goodbye. And he really meant it.

Back at his house, he grinned like a cat with a canary as he crawled into bed. A sweet girl like her was just what he needed. As long as David didn't catch wind of it, this could work out perfectly. Someone like her he could trust to keep her promise, at least until the trouble had blown over and he was back in L.A.

He had a feeling he'd just found a new hobby to keep him occupied in lazy old Tennessee.

Six

I can't help it. I always start out with the best of intentions, but then I lose control. It's not my fault. Why do they have to be so infuriating? Always trying to get what's rightfully mine. It's not fair. So I don't play fair. I break into their homes – it's easy for me – and then I sneak behind them. At that point it's easy; just grab the dog's leash – they always keep it near the door – loop it around their fragile neck and pull. Pull until they slump like an empty sack. Easy peasy.

I like to spend time following them, getting to know them, befriending them. It's like working for the enemy. Except I don't work for them, I just stalk them. After all, why not? It's fun; it's actually the best part.

No, not true. The best part is watching them exhale their last breath. I always relive that moment for hours, for days even. I probably should start making videos, but then it would be too dangerous, they could fall in the wrong hands. I am always so careful. I know all the mistakes the amateurs make. I know better.

Nope. No mistakes. They will never suspect me. They will never catch me.

Seven

Melissa hummed a tune as she waltzed toward the garage door, thinking of Wyatt Rogers. Wyatt Rogers. The famous actor. He'd been in her house. He'd sat around her table. He'd been in her *bed*.

Her skin prickled with excitement at the memory. Wow. It'd been, quite simply, the best sex of her life, and it'd been with a man most women only fantasized about. Butterflies swarmed her insides as she recalled the way he'd kissed her, held her, making love to her like she was the only woman on earth.

She couldn't wait to tell the girls at work. They'd simply go berserk with envy.

He'd be back. She felt sure of it. A connection like theirs was rare. She wasn't sure quite what had brought him back to this lazy part of the world, but she was glad he'd been here. Maybe it was fate tying them together. Maybe, after months of a secret courtship, he'd propose, and they'd have a glamorous Hollywood wedding. Her mind whirled with thoughts of the two of them, together, heading off on a glamourous honeymoon to one of his many houses in some secluded paradise. He'd shower her with the best of everything—the best food, the best clothing—and he'd be so in love with her, he'd buy her diamonds, just because. She could kiss this cruddy old broken-down home—this cruddy *life*—goodbye.

She grinned wider as she twisted the doorknob to the garage. Cupcake was still yipping. The second she opened the door, he jumped into her arms.

"I know you want to be my one and only," she said, stroking his fur. "But I think I have another man in my life now."

She set Cupcake down and he raced off to his food dish. As she walked down the hallway toward her bedroom, she could hear him munching on his food in the kitchen.

Her pulse thrummed under her skin as she went to her bedroom and stared at the unmade bed. She took the pillow in her hands and inhaled deeply. It still smelled like his spicy aftershave. Need coiled deep in her abdomen. He'd been so wonderful. So perfect.

She went to the bathroom and ran the water for a bath. That was just what she needed—a nice bubble bath so that she could lie back and fantasize about her glamorous new life. Running the water, she tested it, then turned to the mirror as steam filled the room.

She twirled a lock of her hair and ran a finger down her cheek. She was pretty. Everyone always said so. She'd always thought she was better than everyone in this place.

Now she would prove it.

Slipping off her kimono, she went to dip a toe into the bath when she noticed something.

Cupcake always finished his food in a blink and liked to laze on the furry carpet beside the tub while she took her bath. But he hadn't come back.

She went to the door and peered out. The hallway was dark, so she could barely see the kitchen. She was used to living alone, but for the first time, a tendril of fear skittered down her neck.

"Cupcake?" she called, hoping to hear his reassuring yip.

But she heard nothing.

Grabbing her towel, she wrapped it around her slim body and went to see what the matter was. Maybe he'd been so excited about Melissa's rare company that he'd tired himself out, and was asleep? Yes, that was likely it.

She went to the kitchen and looked at his bed. It was dark, but she could see the surface of it in the shaft of moonlight shining through the skylight. It was empty.

Then she heard a noise coming from the living room. She turned to look inside. The curtains in the living area swayed, and wind whistled through an open window.

When did I open that? she wondered, thinking back.

She couldn't recall.

She had her trusty alarm, so she wasn't worried. She padded across the hardwood floor toward the foyer to check and make sure she'd set it. After all, she'd been so giddy about Wyatt, walking on clouds. She might have forgotten.

Steps from the console, she noticed the red light was blinking.

That meant that the alarm had been disarmed.

Good thing I checked, she thought, tapping the screen. She called out, "Cupcake! Where are you, you rascal?"

As she pressed the code to rearm the alarm system, she heard his yip.

Somehow, it sounded far away again. As if he was back in the garage.

I did let him out of there, she told herself, tapping her head. *I'm not going crazy, am I?*

She turned and headed toward the garage door again, but stopped in her tracks. No, the sound of Cupcake's barking wasn't coming from the garage. It was coming from outside.

How could he have gotten outside? He hated going out in the dark. He wouldn't have gone out there, unless…

She spun around, now on high-alert, frantically scanning the darkness, trying to figure out what was going on.

I'm just overexcited about Wyatt, she told herself, pulling the towel tighter around herself. *Everything is fine. I just need to get a grip.*

She took one step toward the door to turn the lights on when something tight and unyielding slipped around her neck. She gasped, and her hands flew to it, scrabbling for release, but it was far too much for her to fight against. *A leash. Is this… Cupcake's leash? Someone is strangling me with my dog's leash.*

Shock gripped her. Even as her breath left her, it seemed almost too crazy to believe, like some nightmare she'd soon wake up from. She'd lived alone here, for so long. She had no enemies. *Someone wants me dead... why?... who could be doing this to me?*

Only one name came to mind: *Wyatt Rogers.*

But as impossible as it seemed, she simply couldn't imagine anyone else. Her arms flailed uselessly, her bare feet kicked out wildly beneath her. She felt her eyes bulging, her breath choking out of her, her limbs gradually going numb, ceasing to work. She closed her eyes, and the last thing she heard was her precious Cupcake, yipping and scratching at the front door.

Eight

It was just after seven o'clock when Valentina woke up in the coziness of her bed. Late for her; usually she woke with the sun. But now, it was already up, slashing through the blinds.

Another terrible night's sleep, she thought, recalling all of the tossing and turning she'd done until the wee hours. Early morning, and she already felt exhausted from the workout she'd gotten, tumbling around in her bed, trying to get comfortable.

She stretched, yawing as she looked toward the window where the lake's water was just now starting to shine under the sun. Judging by the cloudless sky it was going to be a beautiful day, perfect for the kayak excursion she was planning later.

Kayaking. That would be nice. She needed something to give her back some energy, and the fresh air would do her good. She threw off the sheet, then rushed to feed her impatient dogs, whose paws she could hear padding around downstairs on the hardwood floor. When she appeared at the top landing, they gave her their normal morning greeting, wagging their tails in excitement from their place at the foot of the stairs.

As she went downstairs, her phone buzzed. She expected the usual *Good morning!* text from Jack, but instead, Michelle's name popped up.

Breakfast at the general store at 8:30?

Her stomach grumbled at the thought of the little café's morning assortment of pastries.

Kayaking could wait. An hour for breakfast, along with some friendly banter, was just what she needed. She quickly got ready and texted her friend that she was on her way to her house so that they could take Michelle's car to get there. Valentina didn't mind walking but, like a lot of people there, her friend wasn't particularly fond of walks.

At least she was able to ride her bike to Michelle's house and to enjoy the fresh morning air. It was cool and pleasant this early, and the streets were empty. The road's gravel crunched under the tires of her bike and every so often birds called from the tall trees.

When she reached her friend's house, Valentina didn't even have the time to lean her bike against one of the tall trees that lined the front of Michelle's front lawn. Michelle came running toward her, her usually cheerful face grim and agitated. She was gripping her tablet in her hands.

"You will never believe what happened!" she said in a warning tone, showing Valentina her tablet, opened to the *Herald-Citizen's* front page.

Confused, Valentina grabbed the tablet, letting out a gasp of shock and horror as she scrolled through the news story.

Only a couple days ago, a woman who lived in a nearby gated community not far from Long Lakes had been found dead. According to the report, one of her friends had found the body when she stopped by for a visit. When the woman didn't answer the door, her friend had at first thought that she simply wasn't home, but then she noticed something through the curtains and, upon further inspection, realized that it was a body. When she let herself in with a spare key, she noticed that the woman had been strangled.

"This is terrible," Valentina commented, handing the tablet back to Michelle.

"I know… and so sad too." Michelle shook her head. "And from the article, it looks like the police have no clue who did it."

"Well… they always say that. I'm sure they have a suspect list a mile long. But they don't tell that to the reporters because then the killer would know what they're up to. Right?"

"I guess. But I doubt she has that many enemies! Her friend described her as such a sweet lady. Everyone liked her. It's creepy, isn't it, knowing that there could be a murderer on the loose?"

"Calm down!" Valentina said, giving her friend's shoulder a pat. "I'm sure it's not a serial killer, targeting random women. It's probably a jealous ex-boyfriend or something. I bet they'll catch the killer by the end of the day."

"You think?" Michelle looked doubtful.

"I *know*."

Even so, while Michelle shook her head, closing out the page, a shiver ran down Valentina's spine. After what had happened recently with those drug dealers, she didn't even want to think of another innocent woman being murdered in such a gruesome way. Strangled? Though that indicated a crime of passion, someone caught up in the heat of the moment, she still didn't like to think of anyone capable of such a thing so close to home.

She threw an arm around Michelle's neck and led her to the car. "Come on. Let's go have breakfast. I'm starving."

"All right." The two walked to Michelle's SUV, which was parked in the driveway, Michelle already digging through her purse for her keys. "You're probably right."

Valentina certainly hoped so. Even though it was probably nothing, she should probably tell Jack. She'd been planning to call him to hear how his project in Memphis was going. She should probably tell him about this latest news.

Come to think of it, he hadn't texted her last night, or this morning. That was odd.

She reached into her bag, for her phone. As if she'd read her mind, Michelle asked, "Are you going to tell Jack?"

"I'm not sure yet. I wouldn't want to worry him for nothing."

Michelle nodded and then the two got into her car, and as they drove to the general store, Valentina sent him a *Good morning!* text. Maybe he'd just had a really busy night, working on that project. He'd said it was a headache.

She stared at the phone until they arrived at the little hub of Long Lakes, about a mile down the road, waiting for him to respond. He didn't. Worry fluttered in her stomach.

They decided to sit outside, but Valentina immediately regretted it the moment they stepped out onto the porch and saw Lola and her gang sitting at one of the tables, Lola talking animatedly to her cronies about the murder.

"Valentina! Michelle!" Lola said as soon as she spotted them, motioning them over. "Have you heard the terrible news?"

Valentina and Michelle traded glances and made their way over to them before getting their own table.

"We did, yes. We were just now talking about it, actually," Michelle said.

"Such a tragedy," Lola continued, dramatically putting a hand against her chest.

Michelle nodded. "Sure was. I still can't believe that the police don't have a clue about who did this! It's ridiculous."

"Or maybe they don't want people to know. Maybe it was somebody from around her community and they don't want to cause any panic," Bernice, one of Lola's hangers-on, ventured.

Valentina sat down stiffly.

"You watch too many mystery shows, Bernie," Lola shushed her.

"I know everybody thinks it's a tragedy," Milly, yet another one of her fans, intervened. "And it is, for sure, but I kind of feel like she asked for it, bless her heart."

Michelle gave her a horrified look. "How can you say something like that?"

"I know that it sounds horrible, but I knew that woman because my sister introduced her to me. We hung out a couple of times and, even though I didn't know her that well, I knew her well enough to realize that she did have her fun with all sorts of men, if you know what I mean. Sure enough, one them wasn't happy about having to share her. I bet you she invited the trouble right into her house."

"You're suggesting it's a crime of jealousy?" Michelle asked.

"Maybe." Milly shrugged. "Or maybe she just decided to sleep with the wrong guy. A crazy man. You never can tell these days. All kinds of strange people around."

"Either way," Valentina said, "I don't believe it's respectful to speculate about her death like this."

"You're right, Valentina, we shouldn't speak ill of the dead. But it's not every day that something like this happens around here, and people around these parts are entirely too trusting. If we can use this as a cautionary tale to stop it from happening to more unsuspecting women, I think we should scream it from the rooftops."

Lola clearly couldn't hide her excitement at having such a tasty bone to chew. She smiled with satisfaction as the rest of the girls around the table all nodded in agreement.

Valentina didn't say anything else. She turned and walked inside to get more sugar for her coffee, clenching her fists when she heard Lola saying to the others, "Poor thing… I don't think she's completely recovered from what happened to her yet. She must be so sensitive about these kinds of things. She's a cautionary tale herself, that girl."

She took a deep breath, grabbed the sugar, went outside, and sat down next to her friend, trying her best to enjoy her breakfast and ignore Lola and her friends as they continued their speculation about the dead woman. Luckily, their table was far enough away that they were able to have a pleasant breakfast, anyway.

An hour later, the two friends drove back to Michelle's place.

"You're very quiet," Michelle said. "Is everything okay?"

Valentina sighed, rolling the window down some air. "I'm fine. I'm just a bit worried, that's all."

"I understand. I mean, I don't want to say that Lola is right about that comment that she made but it must be more difficult for you. All that terrible stuff with Warren and Jerry didn't happen that long ago." She shrugged. "I think all of us women who live alone most of the time are going to be a little on edge. But just lock your doors and keep an eye out for anything suspicious, and I bet you we'll be fine."

Valentina started to play with the hem of her shirt. "You think?"

"Absolutely. Like the girls at the general store said, the woman probably invited that trouble into her house. We're safe in here."

Valentina nodded, hoping she was right. "Good… because Lola's right. I don't think I can deal with any more excitement."

"Honestly," Michelle went on, "I don't know what I would have done if I was in your place. You were so brave, honey."

Michelle reached over and gave her hand a quick squeeze. Valentina forced a smile.

"I just hope that the police will solve this quickly. I can't even imagine how her family and friends must feel."

As she said that, her heart raced in her chest. She couldn't help thinking about how she thought she was going to die when Warren put his hands on her. Her thoughts had gone to Beatrice and Jack and to all her friends back in Italy, and she was sure she'd never see them again. At the memory of that hopelessness, her breath hitched.

"I'm sure they will be able to put that monster behind bars." Michelle's voice made her snap out of her thoughts. "I bet they already know who he is and he'll be in jail before the weekend. Mark my words."

She nodded, not totally convinced. If the police weren't able to find anything to identify the murderer when they examined the crime scene the first time, it was unlikely they'd find something later. At least, that was what Jack always told her when the two of them watched thriller movies. He would always complain about how the FBI or different parts of the crime investigation weren't being portrayed accurately. It was very rare for the police to stumble upon some smoking gun in the midst of an investigation that would lead to an arrest.

She shook her head, blaming Jack for this morbid train of thought. Michelle was right, likely. They probably did already have a suspect, but were keeping that information out of the news. It was only a matter of time before the murderer would be brought to justice.

They arrived in front of Michelle's house and Valentina grabbed her bike, feeling the need for a kayak excursion now more than ever.

"If you need to talk, you know I'm here," Michelle reminded her. Valentina thanked her as she jumped on her bike and rode back home.

As soon as she returned there, she quickly changed into her kayak gear and was soon paddling placidly on the lake.

Before she even made it out to the center, the silence and calm that surrounded her were already helping to soothe her. She stopped in the middle of the lake, putting a hand in the water to enjoy its coolness, while the sun grew warmer and warmer on her bare arms.

At that moment, she regretted being in such a rush that she totally forgot to put sunblock on; even if it was just October, the sun was hitting pretty hard.

All around the lake, it was just so beautiful. The houses resting on the lakeshore were like a picture postcard, and the water was calm and so clean that she could see the fish swimming rapidly near the surface. There was a gentle breeze that every so often caressed the water, creating very small waves and offering some relief from the sun's warmth. The air smelled like wood and she could hear people talking and laughing loudly from one of the house's porches. The leaves were starting to change and they were sporting bold shades of yellow, orange and red. Who needed New England for foliage-watching when her own slice of paradise was right outside her front door?

Valentina looked back at her house, feeling so proud of herself for all that she accomplished on her own.

Antonio had left her not long after they bought that home, and everybody back in Italy thought she was crazy for deciding to stay anyway and to take on the wine importation company all by herself. But she was never one to quit.

Besides, her daughter was already settling in by then, and she couldn't just bring her back to Italy.

So she stayed, kept the house, kept the company and rocked it, and now she couldn't have been happier about her choice, especially because otherwise she would never have met Jack. The thought of making it through these last few months without him was an idea she didn't even want to contemplate.

She smiled to herself, and her happy thoughts made her wonder what she could make for lunch. While she was contemplating a simple pasta with leeks, accompanied by a nice glass of Vermentino, she noticed somebody standing on one of the docks, waving at her.

She shielded her eyes with her hand and squinted, still unable to recognize the person.

Only when she looked at the house behind the mysterious silhouette did she realize that it was the actor who had rented Firefly Cabin. Wyatt Rogers.

She looked around for a second, thinking he couldn't possibly be waving at her, but there was no one else around, so she started to slowly paddling closer to his dock, until they were able to hear each other.

"Sorry to bother you," the man immediately said, "But I've noticed you around here a couple of times and I thought I could introduce myself. I'm Wyatt—"

"Rogers. I know."

He smiled. "I guess I wasn't able to maintain the secret that long."

Valentina laughed, thinking that he was quite handsome. He was tall, with thick, dark hair, fashionable stubble, and big, dark eyes. His shoulders were large, his arms very muscular. His cheekbones were very sharp, his lips full and his nose straight and small. Definitely a movie star. No wonder Hollywood had taken to him.

"It isn't every day a movie star moves into Long Lakes. You're the talk of the town, Mr. Rogers. I'm Valentina."

"Valentina? Is that Italian?"

"How did you guess?"

"I've been to Italy a couple of times. Beautiful country, can't wait to visit again, and the food was unreal."

"Yeah… Our food always leaves a mark."

He offered her that perfect dimpled smile of his again, before looking around the lake. "So, you're the sporty type?"

"I like to think so, yeah."

"I love sports myself, even if I have to admit that I usually prefer the gym to Mother Nature."

Valentina laughed, then indicated the house with her chin. "How are you liking the place? You're renting there, yes?"

"Oh, the house is amazing! Can't say all this quiet suits me though, even if I needed it. Work has been crazy lately."

"I bet. You're from…?"

"Originally from this area. But I've been living in L.A. for the past decade. Ever been?"

She shook her head, thinking about Beatrice and her reaction once she told her about this exceptional encounter.

"Well," Wyatt continued, "If you ever decide to visit there, don't hesitate to let me know. I would love to show you around."

"I'll keep that in mind."

She was about to say goodbye and keep kayaking, but then he asked her more questions: why she moved to the States, how long she had been there and whether she liked it better than her own country. Valentina patiently answered all his questions, even though she really wanted to get going. She still wanted to kayak some more, plus lunchtime was approaching and she was starting to feel very hungry.

However, Wyatt didn't seem to want to let her go. She got the feeling he was very bored, and just looking for someone to be friends with. He kept talking and talking to the point where Valentina had to interrupt him. "I'm sorry, but I need to go."

"Oh, of course. I wouldn't want to keep you if you're busy," Wyatt said, raking his hands through his hair. "But I would like to ask you out so that we could chat some more. I always enjoy the company of a lovely woman such as yourself."

Now Valentina blushed. Beatrice would absolutely *die* if she heard this one.

"I'm flattered, Mister Rogers, but I'm afraid I can't accept that."

"Not even if it was just for a kayak excursion? Nothing serious,

I would just like to spend some time with somebody. Anybody. It can be quite boring for a city boy around here."

Valentina thought about it, wondering if he really had no ulterior motives or if Jack would have any problems with it. No, he was a famous movie star. Of course he didn't want to date her. She understood that he probably had so much company in Hollywood—this seclusion was probably a shock to his system. All he wanted was a friend.

And she could be that. If he did turn serious, she could always tell him no. "All right. Sure. Why not?"

"Good. Why don't we meet this weekend for kayaking? I've always wanted to do it."

She smiled. "Sure. Sounds great."

It was pretty late now, so she went back to her house, but she could still feel his eyes following her from the deck. Once again, she wondered if it was wise to accept; after all, she didn't know the guy or whether he had been honest when he told her that he just needed some company. But it was done, so she could only hope he wouldn't get the wrong impression.

Besides, how many times would she get the chance to converse with a famous actor? Her friends and family in Italy seemed to think that she schmoozed with movie stars in America all the time. Now she really could. This would definitely be a story she could tell them for a long time to come, a definitive American Experience.

At home she made her lunch of pasta with leeks, sat down with her glass of wine, and then decided to video call Jack.

Nine

Jack was sitting at a café, sipping coffee while staring at the busy road in front of him. It was a cooler day; a sharp wind kept hitting the trees and the people ,who would brace themselves in their jackets while big, threating clouds crossed the sky. Despite the cold, Jack decided to sit outside.

He had other things on his mind.

Goddamn that Dees.

His business trip in Memphis had just gone from bad to worse. He'd been getting ready this morning, bright and early, ready to tackle the Memphis Brokerage for good and find the missing pieces to the puzzle, when he'd gotten that call from his supervisor.

"You're not working to our satisfaction," Dees had said. "We'd expected more in the way of results by now."

"But I—"

"You just need fresh eyes on the paper," his boss had said. Dees wasn't one to soften the blow, but that was the closest he'd ever gotten. "We can't afford to dick around with this case until I retire, Erikson."

He'd tried to explain, but Dees didn't give him the chance.

"Expect Franklin Watts to be there tomorrow afternoon," he'd grumbled, and then hung up before Jack could even think of protesting.

Not that a protest would've done any good. Dees made a decision, and stuck with it. But Franklin Watts? The sniveling, obnoxious little kiss-ass was like teacher's pet in the department. He lived to prove himself, and make other people look bad in the process.

No, this wasn't going to be a good day. And once word got around at the field office that Dees decided to assign him a partner after his constant failures, as if he were a damn rookie? He'd never hear the end of it.

As if that wasn't frustrating enough, when he'd tried to vent about it to Valentina, she hadn't answered the phone. So he'd sent her a text, but that didn't seem to convey how upset he was. She made light of it. She seemed to think that it wasn't that big of a deal, which only made things worse. She said that she understood why he might have been mad about it, but that maybe he needed to see this in a less negative light and consider it a way to get some stress off of his shoulders.

And Valentina was still worrying him a lot. He still felt as if she was becoming more and more distant but he didn't have the guts to tell her.

He learned a long time ago that not dealing with issues or doubts in a relationship is the worst idea one could have and yet he still refused to talk to her about his concerns, for fear of sounding too needy.

He was actually about to see if she had texted him when he received a video call from her.

"Hey."

"Hey, baby. I was just thinking about you," he said.

"Aww…"

He smiled, taking another sip of his coffee, admiring how pretty she was sitting on her porch, with the sunlight on her face. But was it him, or did she look a little distracted? She kept looking off-screen, at something. Was she with someone?

"Are you alone?" he asked.

She laughed. "Of course. I just got done with lunch. I'm sitting out on the back porch. It's a gorgeous day."

He wished he could be there with her, on that deck, looking out at Firefly Lake. He'd never really known what peace was until he'd found that place. Those nights where he and Valentina would sit out on the dock, watching the sun slip behind the trees… he longed for that right now. He bet the leaves, changing color, would be a sight to behold.

"Sounds nice." He couldn't keep the bitterness out of his voice.

"How are you holding up? You're still pissed about that guy coming over there tomorrow?"

Jack's smile immediately turned into a very disappointed smirk. "Yeah… I know I should get over it but I can't help it. I really don't like the idea."

"It's understandable, but maybe working with somebody won't be that bad."

"We'll see about that, I guess."

He said that just because he knew that she thought that he was kind of overreacting about this but in reality it was going to be bad for him. He didn't like to work with others and he didn't like the idea of his boss thinking that he wasn't good enough on his own.

"Everything will work itself out. You'll see. I actually have some news myself," Valentina went on.

Even through the screen Jack could notice that her entire body seemed to tense all of a sudden and her tone changed too, becoming way more serious that it was just a second before.

"What news?"

"A woman that lived just outside Long Lakes was murdered a few days ago."

"What?" He said it so loud that a couple walking past him glanced at him, curious.

He actually squeezed the cup of coffee so much that some of it splashed out of it on his hand.

"Son of a bitch!" he cussed, quickly grabbing a napkin to dry his hand.

"You're okay?" Valentina asked.

"Yeah, yeah, I'm fine, just spilled some coffee on myself but it doesn't matter. Are you all right? I mean…"

She looked down for a second before answering and he could tell that she was not okay but being the stubborn and proud woman that she was, she didn't want to admit that, not even to him.

"Yeah, I… I'm okay but I'm kind of concerned because the

police still don't know who did it or why. At least, that's what they're saying."

Jack immediately felt shivers down his spine and told her that she needed to be extra careful, that he would never forgive himself if something happened to her but she simply told him to not be dramatic.

How could he not be though? He'd already risked losing her once, he could not allow that to ever happen again.

Valentina must have realized how worried he was getting because she changed the subject, smiling in a way that didn't quite reach her eyes.

"Something else happened," she said.

"If it was another murder, I swear…"

She laughed, "Nothing like that. I just happened to have a chit chat with that famous actor who's staying here at Long Lakes!"

Jack raised an eyebrow, thinking that she must have been joking just to lighten up the conversation after the horrible news that she'd just told him. There was no way an actor would even spend a day at that place.

"You're messing with me," he said, laughing.

"I'm not! I'd heard rumors about this guy staying at Firefly Cabin but I didn't think I would meet him. His name's Wyatt Rogers."

"Oh…"

"Have you heard of him?"

"No. You know me and Hollywood. You actually met him?"

"Yep."

He gritted his teeth. He could already feel the green monster popping up, but he tried his best to keep his voice light and unconcerned. "How did you guys end up meeting then?"

"Oh, I was kayaking around the lake when he noticed me from his deck and we just started talking. It was funny, he actually kept asking me a bunch of questions and didn't let me go for a good five minutes. He even asked me to go kayaking with him this weekend."

"Ah…" The word erupted from his mouth before he had a chance to control the way it came out.

"You don't sound thrilled."

She was right. He wasn't. He'd been worried that she'd been losing interest in him, but now it seemed like whatever interest she'd once had in him was completely lost. Why else would she accept an invitation from a guy who was clearly flirting with her? An undoubtedly handsome and charming actor, on top of that!

Also, why the hell was that guy there, in Long Lakes, of all the places in the world? It was like the universe was trying to play tricks on him to see how much he could handle before he completely lost it.

But as hard as it was to stomach, he managed to joke, "Just making sure you're not falling in love with someone behind my back."

She laughed. "Oh, don't you worry about that. I don't give away my heart so easily."

At least he'd managed to strike the right tone. She'd thought it was a joke. Even though there was a definite vein of seriousness behind it. And she was right about giving away her heart. Even now, months into their relationship, he still wasn't sure he fully had hers.

"Hey, listen, I gotta go now but I'll call you back as soon as I can, okay?" he added then, not wanting Valentina to notice how irritated he was getting.

"Okay, love you." She said it almost dismissively. Like the way most people ended conversations, almost without thinking. It made his bad mood worse.

"Love you, too, and remember, be careful, please."

"I will."

Once he hung up, he threw the rest of his coffee in the trash and started walking around, nervous. He started to think that maybe it would have been best to just hand the case to Franklin and tell him to have at it, while he went back to Valentina.

The thought was tempting. Of course, she'd be suspicious as to why he'd suddenly given up the job. But he didn't have to say it was about the pompous actor hitting on her. He could blame it on his concern over the murder in the nearby development, explain he didn't think she should be alone.

But if she was already thinking about replacing him with someone famous and more sophisticated than him, his being there in person wouldn't make any difference. The relationship would be doomed to fail, no matter what he did.

No, he thought to himself, Valentina was not the type of woman to engage in flights of fancy like that. She wasn't like Yvonne, and that's why he'd fallen for her so quickly, when he'd previously sworn off ever getting into another relationship.

But those doubts did not leave his mind for the rest of the day. As a result, he found very little in the files from Memphis Brokerage, and went to bed with a headache. Sadness, nervousness and all those damn doubts hung over him like a fog, and they kept him awake almost the entire night.

Ten

Valentina sat quietly on her front porch, hidden by the railing, reading a book. From here she could just see the very tip of Firefly Cabin, peeking out from behind the trees.

But she wasn't looking for Wyatt Rogers.

She was patiently waiting for her *other* new friends to show up. A doe had just had two adorable fawns and her yard was their favorite place to hang out after dusk, so she had started to leave grains and even some hay that she brought from the barn. She was delighted to see that the mama and the babies were thoroughly enjoying those unexpected gifts, but so far, she hadn't seen much of them.

She could not let the dogs keep her company during these stakeouts, because they would have scared the deer family away in their excitement. She knew they didn't mean to harm the deer, but they could not suppress their hunting instinct.

It was almost dark; twilight was her favorite time of the day, and it was getting hard to see among the lush woods surrounding her log home. But she could clearly hear the deer cautiously approaching the spot where she used to leave them food; it was a small stretch of grass more clearly visible from her vantage point.

She waited a few more minutes, and finally her patience was rewarded; three silhouettes – one bigger and two smaller – moved out of the dark protection of the woods and approached their feeding spot. Valentina grabbed her binoculars and was able to vaguely see the three deer happily munching on their treats.

After less than five minutes, it was already too dark to see anything at all, but she could still hear them rustling around.

She loved these sightings; they made her feel part of nature, which she loved passionately. Antonio used to make fun of her because she was what he spitefully called a "green." Yes, she was an environmentalist, but she couldn't see what was wrong with that. She wished more people were more ecofriendly; the rate this world was going, the next generation wouldn't have enough resources to feed the alarmingly increasing world population, not to mention the increasing number of animal species that were on the brink of extinction or already extinct.

So she enthusiastically and scrupulously recycled all her plastic, paper, cans and metal, although Tennessee was one of the least ecofriendly states in a country that was already heavily burdened with a disproportionate resource consumption. Still, she wanted to be a good example for her daughter, who represented the next generation, and never stopped her "green" habits, despite Antonio's mocking.

Now this little deer family filled her heart with joy; just watching these creatures in their natural habitat was a privilege for Valentina, and she thoroughly enjoyed these brief moments. She realized that when she was younger she had chosen the wrong course of study and line of work; she should have followed her predisposition and studied zoology or ethology. She would now be happily working among animals and her heart would maybe feel more at peace. Instead, she chose languages and she fell in love with English and the United States. She didn't regret her life choices, but there was this little place in her heart that kept pulling at her anytime she was in close contact with nature and its inhabitants.

Dante and Luna were the only animals she could share her life with, but living in Long Lakes had often given her the chance to observe many interesting animals, most of which either did not exist in Italy or were not as plentiful. Deer, coyote, raccoons, beavers, possums, eagles, bears, not to mention the less pleasant ones, such as skunks and venomous snakes. The last two she mostly kept away from for obvious reasons, but at least she wasn't hell-bent on killing them first chance she got, like some of her neighbors.

That was one more thing she liked about Jack; he never made fun of her when she turned to mush anytime she met a dog, kitten, horse or any animal that moved her heart. Most women her age behaved like that in front of children, whereas she much preferred animals. In fact, she didn't bat an eye when her daughter Beatrice recently announced, in a rather flat tone, that she would never have kids. She was still very young and she hadn't developed any motherly instincts yet, but Valentina wouldn't cry a river over a lack of grandkids; Bea was entitled to live a childless life, even if it would probably feel a little lonely in her old age.

Jack was a good man. But that afternoon, during their call, she'd hurt him. She'd brought out the jealousy in him. She couldn't blame him for being worried. He'd been hurt, just as she had been.

"Yooo hoooo!"

She reluctantly emerged from her wandering thoughts; she saw Lola, her brash neighbor, walking up the driveway toward her.

Valentina sighed at the interruption, but forced a smile as she closed her book. It was too dark to read, anyway. "Hello, Lola. What brings you here tonight?"

"Oh, just making the rounds," she said, collapsing on the wood bench on Valentina's porch. "Seeing what's new with everyone. What's the scoop?"

Of course, Lola had a purpose for her appearance. Either she was in need of some good gossip, or she needed something else. But Valentina was the wrong person for gossip. She kept her lips tight, especially around the likes of Lola. She knew that anything she told Lola or her crew would likely make the rounds in Long Lakes at lightning speed. "I don't have much going on. What about you?"

It was at that moment Valentina noticed the clipboard in Lola's hands. Lola wasn't paying attention, though. She was leaning over the railing, craning her neck toward Firefly Cabin.

"Hello? Lola?"

Lola coughed and looked at her. "Oh. I'm sorry. I was just noticing. You have quite the view of that Hollywood heart-throb's place, don't you?" She squinted back at the place. "Have any good sightings? Any juicy gossip? You know, you could take pictures for the paparazzi and make a *fortune!*"

Valentina shook her head. "It's too far away for me. And I'm not too interested in whatever he's up to." She pointed to the clipboard. "What's that all about?"

Lola held it up and said, "Well, I'm sure you heard, with all that to-do with Warren, they needed a new HOA president. I was filling in only temporarily, but I guess the board thought I was doing such a good job, they made it permanent."

"Oh. Congratulations."

She beamed. "Yes, well, it's quite a responsibility, you know, but I've been doing what I can. But I'm sure you've been dealing with the latest problem. You understand, it simply cannot stand. It's right in our Long Lakes contracts!"

Valentina stared, confused. "I'm sorry… what is?"

"About renting out properties in Long Lakes to strangers. It isn't allowed!" she said, tsking. "It first came to my attention with Jack. But obviously, that was a good thing, since he turned out to be a Fed. But with Wyatt Rogers… that's another thing entirely. And now that new English chap?"

"I don't know what you're talking about?"

She pointed in the opposite direction to Wyatt's house. "The Englishman. He's very queer. I think he moved in yesterday? In the old Barnes place."

"Oh!" The Barnes couple were older, and had passed away last year. The house had stood empty for a long time. The weeds and vegetation had slowly come to swallow up the place. She hadn't noticed any activity in the home at all. Of course, she had to admit, much of her attention had been focused the opposite, way, toward Firefly Cabin and Wyatt Rogers. She wondered if Michelle knew about this. "I didn't know."

"Well, we'll be bringing it up at the next board meeting. I'm proposing that any potential renter must get approval in writing from the board. And I'm also circulating a petition to get a couple more guards on duty."

"Guards?" she asked, taking the clipboard from Lola and squinting to read. It was getting too dark to see much, but she already saw an impressive register of signatures, Michelle's included.

"Yes, well, you know we have Joe and Tom at the front gates. But I want to get a few temporary guards to patrol the area. Just for next six months or so." She leaned in. "Because of, you know."

Valentina nodded. "That poor girl's murder outside the development?"

"Not only that, but with strangers in the development now… you never know what might happen. Plus," now she leaned in even closer and her voice fell to a whisper, "some people have reported seeing strange things."

"Strange things?"

She nodded. "Ellie said she saw a blonde girl. Thought it was a ghost. You know Ellie, bless her heart. She's a little—" She twirled a finger near her head. "But there have been other sightings. Someone creeping around, peering in windows."

A chill went down Valentina's spine. "Really? I didn't realize."

"I tell you, I think it's the paparazzi. Trying to get a handle on that Hollywood hunk." She shrugged. "Joe and Tom do what they can at the front gate, but anyone can come in around the perimeter. You know we don't have fences. So it's not a good thing."

Valentina had to admit, this was one thing she agreed with Lola about. She quickly signed her name.

"Thank you very much, ma'am," Lola said, tipping an imaginary hat as she took the clipboard back. "I tell you, as exciting as it is to have a bit of Hollywood here, I don't know if it's so good. If this had come in front of the board, I would've pooh-poohed it before you could say Jack Robinson."

Of course, as she said her goodbyes and stepped to the edge of the porch, she couldn't help glancing over at the famous resident's home.

Valentina watched her go to the road, jump on her giant tricycle with the powerful headlight, and pedal away. She realized that she couldn't hear any more rustling, which meant that the doe and her fawns had finished dinner and left.

It was now completely dark, and she was alone.

And somewhere out there is a murderer. Someone who killed a woman in cold blood.

And maybe a creepy stalker, too…

She swallowed, and a chill went down her spine. Not for the first time, she wished Jack was here with her.

Don't be silly, she told herself. *You're fine. Everything is fine.*

Yawning, she decided to call it a night. As she retreated to her front door, she took one last glance into the darkness for the deer. Leaning over the railing she could see Firefly Cabin, silhouetted by the still-light sky. A single light blazed from a window. Wyatt Rogers was there, and she wondered if he was thinking about their upcoming kayaking trip, or if he'd forgotten about it entirely, considering he was an important person, with places to go and people to see.

At first, she thought she saw the deer, lurking among the tree line to the right of the Firefly Cabin. But then, as she willed her eyes to focus, she realized the shape was not that of an animal.

It looked suspiciously human.

A trick of the eye, she told herself.

Sure enough, when she blinked again, it was gone.

Her body quaked. Hugging herself, she went back inside her house and locked the door after her. So what if the dogs barked and woke her? She decided, right then, that that was a good thing.

Eleven

Two days after he saw Valentina, Wyatt was nearly out of his mind—antsy.

During the intervening forty-eight hours, he'd jogged around the house a thousand times. Worked out in the private gym until his muscles ached. Took long baths. Swam in the lake. Made a few gourmet meals. Tried to read a book. Rode up and down the street on an old bicycle he found, looking for action.

But there was none in the godforsaken place.

If David expected him to survive out here without any of his usual fun and games, he was sorely mistaken.

And Valentina…

He'd call her, of course, for "kayaking."

She was older than he was. Not much. A hair. But older women were good. They were realistic, knew what they wanted. Usually just sex. None of that other stuff. They didn't indulge in childish fantasies of happily ever after.

She seemed like she would be a tough one to get to know. She wasn't as easy as most American women. But he'd get her. The key was not calling right away. Three days. That was the rule. He'd give it another day, and she'd be eating out of the palm of his hand.

But today… dull, dull, dull. Excruciating.

Throwing up his hands, he decided to pay a visit to the general store. He didn't really know what else to do, but at least there he could get something for lunch.

He even walked there, trying to enjoy some fresh air. The little pebbles on the road crunched under the only pair of sports shoes that he owned, and he tried not to think about how dirty the dust would make them. That was one thing about this place. There was dust everywhere. It wasn't like L.A., where, in his wealthy little corner of Beverly Hills, his drivers and entourage provided a safe little bubble so he could avoid the nastiness.

It was a cloudy day. The sky looked gray and angry and the scent of rain gently caressed the air. It looked like it would open up at any moment and drench him, but it didn't. He made the entire mile-long walk without wrecking his perfect hair.

When he entered the general store, the smell of wood immediately surrounded him. It was midday, and the place was relatively empty. The pretty lady at the cash register smiled widely at him. He had been there a couple of times before, despite it being a threat to his secrecy, and every time he walked in, she always lit up.

"How are you doing today, Mr. Rogers?" she asked, coyly tucking a lock of her blonde hair behind her ear.

"Pretty good, Ellie. What about yourself?" he said, pouring on his trademark charm. Young, pretty, and stacked. She'd be fun, but she wouldn't be a conquest. She was married, and probably wouldn't need coaxing to jump into the sack with him.

He could be spending the night with her. All he had to do was say the word.

"Oh, I'm great, thank you! What can I help you with?" She leaned forward, eager to assist.

He considered it. One night with her, and she'd probably turn *Fatal Attraction* on him. He'd known plenty of women like that. And now, he had to be even more careful. A woman like Ellie would probably tell half of Tennessee she'd slept with him by the following morning. No thanks. He couldn't risk it.

"You have any salads? I thought I'd get one and eat it out on the deck overlooking the lake."

She nodded. "Sure! That sounds nice! Caesar or Garden?

They're in the fridge over in that corner." She pointed to the back of the store. "I can get you one if you want?"

He waved a hand at her. "Not at all. I can get it."

He went to the back of the store and grabbed a small, sad, wilted salad and a package of balsamic vinaigrette, then went to the front and set it down, together with a pack of gum.

"So how has the day been treating you?" he asked her as he fished his wallet out of his jeans.

"Oh. I'm just thinking up pie recipes for the Pikeville Annual Fall Festival. It's next Saturday. You going?"

He winced. *I would rather be dead.* "I wasn't planning on it."

"Well, it's a big deal around these parts. I've made the best cherry pie for their annual bake-off three years running. Out of thirty-six entries!"

"Imagine that…" he said, leaning forward, humoring her.

"Yes. But I think I might want to switch it up and try blueberry. You like pie? Maybe I could bring some by for you to try before the big event?"

"That sounds like it'd be…" He trailed off as his eyes roved to the magazine rack at the checkout.

She went on talking about her pies, but he wasn't listening anymore. A picture on the newspaper on the rack at checkout caught his attention instead. He grabbed one to get a closer look. The picture of Melissa was taking the whole front page of the newspaper, and the headline *Brutal murder in a gated community near Pikeville* made his heart beat in his chest like a hammer. As he read the article, his knees wobbled and a cold sweat broke out on his forehead.

"What is this all about?" he interrupted Ellie, trying his best to sound nonchalant.

"Oh! It's so sad…" Ellie said, resting a hand on her heart. "The police still don't have any idea who killed the poor woman."

Wyatt bit his bottom lip as his fingers gripped the newspaper.

"Anyway," she continued, "If you want, I can bring it by this afternoon, and—"

"How much for the paper?"

She paused. Her face reddened. "The paper? Just a dollar."

He went through his wallet before slapping a dollar on the counter.

"I hope it doesn't give you a bad impression of our little home," Ellie said with a giggle. "Really, we're all very nice people here in Long Lakes. This has never happened before."

"It hasn't?" He stared until Melissa's grainy photograph was burned into his retinas.

"No. Oh, well…" She giggled a little more. "There was a little murder mystery that happened earlier this year. But thank goodness for Jack."

His eyes shot to hers. "Jack?"

"I wonder if Valentina already told Jack about all of this. I'm sure she has," Ellie went on, as Wyatt stared at her, confused.

"Valentina?"

Ellie nodded. "She's an Italian lady who lives here. Kind of tight-lipped and mysterious, to be honest. Not one of us, really. Her boyfriend, Jack, works for the FBI. He actually solved a crime right here in the community last year. It was such a horrible mess! Drugs and murders and frauds. It was *insane!*"

Once again, Ellie went on rambling by herself, while her words resonated in Wyatt's head. *Valentina has a boyfriend who works for the FBI.* Now he could clearly feel a drop of sweat running down his forehead. He quickly swiped at it and interrupted Ellie.

"Is this Jack around here?"

"Oh, no, I believe he's in Memphis at the moment. At least, that's what Lola says, and Lola knows everyone's comings and goings. But geez, I wish he were here! I'd feel a lot safer with an FBI agent here, especially knowing there's some psycho killing innocent women roaming around free."

Shit. Wyatt scanned the exit. *Nice move, Wyatt. How do you keep getting yourself into these things?*

He took a deep, cleansing breath, and quickly said goodbye to

Ellie, who gave him a confused look as he rushed out of the store. He practically ran back home, where he paced the living room floor, still clenching the newspaper.

He'd read it again a couple of times as he walked, wondering what the hell to do next. Then it dawned on him that he had the perfect solution right under his nose: Valentina.

Figuring out where her house was based on its position on the lake, he immediately got into his car and slowly drove around until he recognized it. It wasn't hard to find. It was neat and well taken care of, exactly the type of home he expected a woman like Valentina to keep. It had a little placard atop the front door that said, *Elsewhere.*

As soon as he knocked, he heard barks from the other side of the door and his mouth folded into a grimace. He hated dogs. Actually, all animals. And they didn't like him much, either.

Soon after, he heard a voice inside speaking in Italian, and Valentina opened the door. She clearly wasn't expecting anybody since she was dressed very casually, with her hair in a ponytail and a cup of coffee in her hand.

And she has an FBI boyfriend, he thought, gritting his teeth. No wonder she'd seemed reluctant to accept his offer to go kayaking before.

"Mr. Rogers…" she said, putting a leg in front of her over-agitated dogs. "Nice to see you. What can I do for you?"

"I'm so sorry to bother you," he said, collecting himself, "But I wanted to ask you if we could schedule our kayaking excursion? I know we made rough plans, but I really can't do *rough*. My agent just called me and told me I need to work on a script for a new series. I'm sure I'll be quite busy for a while, and if I don't put it on my calendar now, I'm afraid I'll never get the chance to get out there."

She seemed a little confused, but in the end nodded. "Oh, sure. I don't see the problem. When would you like to meet?"

"Would this afternoon be a good time for you?"

Her eyes widened in surprise. She hesitated, turning toward the open laptop on the porch table.

"I'm sure I can cut myself some time for that," she finally said and Wyatt smiled.

"Perfect! What do you say we meet around four?"

"Works for me!"

He said goodbye to her and walked up to his car, feeling slightly relieved; the first part of his plan had worked.

Once home, he ate his terrible, wilted salad on the deck as planned, watching Valentina's house carefully and fine-tuning his plan in his head. Feeling he had everything under control, he even managed an hour's catnap on the plush sofa.

That afternoon, while driving toward Valentina's home, he smiled. He'd never been kayaking before, but it wouldn't be a problem. He was naturally good at everything he did. Plus, she looked like a pro and could probably teach him. That could create plenty of time for togetherness.

Valentina was waiting for him on her dock, her two red kayaks already in the water, ready to go. She waved at him, smiling, and he smiled back. She easily boarded her kayak, but when Wyatt put a foot on his, he was uncertain and unstable. Valentina looked at him with an amused smile on her face.

"First time, huh?" she said, chuckling slightly.

"Yeah… How did you guess?"

She laughed as he was finally able to sit down. The two of them paddled the lake, Valentina offering gentle pointers now and then, until she looked up at the sky.

"I'm afraid we won't be able to stay out too long," she said. "Looks like it will rain soon."

"What a shame," he said, feigning disappointment. He had been on the damn thing for only a minute and it was already getting on his nerves.

As they were slowly moving around the lake, surrounded by silence, interrupted only by the splish-splosh of their paddles or by the birds' chirps, he asked her more questions about herself, until he got the conversation where he really wanted it.

"So, I've heard that your boyfriend is a Fed. Is that true? Or is it just one of the many rumors that get spread around here?"

She looked surprised for a split second, but then nodded and explained that yes, her boyfriend did work for the FBI and he was currently in Memphis, working on a fraud case. "But he said he should be coming out this way soon. More business he has in this area. Some big case he's working on."

"That's very interesting," he said nonchalantly, trying to appear as calm and unaffected as possible. "Must be exciting to have a partner in law enforcement, uh?"

Valentina shrugged. "Sometimes."

She didn't elaborate, and he gathered she didn't want to talk about it anymore, so they spent the rest of the tour exchanging only a few words every so often, until small rain drops started to fall. They decided to head back, which they did just in time; the moment they reached the dock, the skies opened up, the rain coming down angrily.

"I meant to ask you," Wyatt said while he lifted the kayak on land, "I'd love to have dinner with you, if you're ever willing? I've heard that you're an astonishing cook and I'd love to try your food."

"Astonishing? Who told you that?" She seemed embarrassed.

"Word gets around these small communities, I guess." He flashed her his most charming smile.

"Well—"

"How about tonight?"

She seemed reluctant to run with the idea, with good reason. She had a boyfriend.

But boyfriends had never stopped him before.

"Just as friends. Of course." He remembered her wine business and added, "I'm very passionate about wine; I'd love to try some of yours."

He could tell that he hit a soft spot; the woman clearly loved her wines. "Well, I guess I could prepare something quick."

Wyatt's smile widened and she told him to follow her into the house. He followed her and stood in the mudroom, dripping, until she returned with some towels.

"Oh, we're soaked!" she said with a laugh.

He peeled off his shirt, since he knew the sight of his chest was irresistible to most women. And he needed Valentina to be putty in his hands, if he was going to do what he had planned.

Toweling off, he noticed with some satisfaction the blush that crept over her cheeks as she avoided the view.

She stepped backwards. "I'll take a shower and then I'll think of something to make."

"That sounds awesome. I really appreciate it, Valentina."

She smiled politely before telling him to get comfortable and then heading up to the bathroom.

As soon as she closed the bathroom's door behind herself, he walked up to the kitchen counter where she left her phone, just like he'd hoped she would. Just his luck, it wasn't locked. He scrolled through it quickly, focusing on the messages between her and this Fed boyfriend, Jack.

Of course, she'd just written to him only an hour before. Mostly boring shit. A lot of *How's your day—fine—miss you—love you* crap that meant nothing to him. There were a few interesting messages, though. From it, he gleaned that Jack was in Memphis for an undetermined length of time, working on a case, and that he was failing miserably at it.

Wyatt's mouth quirked into a smile at that.

The water upstairs was still rushing, so he quickly got to work. He'd done all this stuff in his college days, and had been the favorite in his fraternity at UT because he was able to give all his brothers ways of tracking their girlfriends via their phone. One-two-three seconds later, he'd expertly installed a spy app to make sure he'd be able to keep an eye on her every time he wanted. He couldn't take any risks, he had to make sure that this Jack guy wasn't going to get suspicious about him.

Even though Jack seemed like a total idiot.

Wyatt quickly put the phone down and sat on the couch, trying his best to ignore the two dogs that kept trying to sniff his pants and cuddle with him. He really wanted to slap their intrusive muzzles, but he was deterred by the size of their teeth.

Not too long after that, Valentina was back downstairs, her hair wet, wearing a loose tunic and leggings that made her look younger. She'd taken some care in her appearance, he decided, which was a good sign.

She peeked in the fridge. "I'm thinking risotto with shrimp and zucchini and a Cialla Bianco?"

"Sounds perfect." Wyatt did not lie when he'd said that he loved wines. Even if he was no expert, he did know some of them. Cialla Bianco was an excellent wine.

They chatted as she stirred the risotto. She poured him a little bit of wine every so often but he was distracted. He kept thinking about the dead girl, Melissa, and about Valentina's boyfriend's position in the FBI.

He kept glancing quickly at her phone and every time she grabbed it to check something, he got a little bit agitated. He was really good with technology, so it was unlikely she'd notice anything different, but he still couldn't believe that he'd got tangled up in this mess in no time. *It's like I can't get away from it.*

Before that day, everything seemed to be going fine, but now everything was ten times worse, and if his plan to limit the damage didn't work, he could end up in prison for a very, *very* long time.

Dinner was finally ready and Valentina kept asking him a bunch of questions about show biz, about the new script that he lied about and about the last series that he worked on. He ate the food with pleasure and patiently answered all her questions, deciding that he definitely needed to see her again to take advantage of the fact that her boyfriend wasn't there, so he could keep an even closer eye on her.

And maybe even get the idiot boyfriend out of the way for good. That shouldn't be too hard. Valentina clearly liked him. And any time he put on his charm, most women were powerless. He just had to find an in.

"So," he blurted, "did you hear about that poor woman that got killed around here?"

Valentina's eyes widened.

"Yes," she answered. "I believe everybody already knows about her."

"I wonder if the police will find anything soon."

"I certainly hope so… What happened to her was terrible."

"It really was. But maybe your boyfriend could help with the investigation once he gets back."

Valentina cleaned her mouth with a napkin, still looking pretty nervous. "He doesn't work on homicides. He only takes care of fraud cases."

"Oh… I was told he solved a pretty hot case here."

"He wasn't supposed to."

Now her voice sounded strained. She got up to collect the dishes from the table to put them in the dishwasher.

"I'm sorry. I didn't mean to upset you."

"It's okay… I… I just don't like to talk about what happened here."

"I understand. Well… I'm sure you must be on edge. What with a murderer being on the loose."

Her eyes went to his. She sucked in a breath but said nothing.

"If you need anything, I'm just next door," he said, giving her his most charming smile. "I'll be there. Just call me. Any time of night or day. All right?"

He'd hoped she'd get the hint, invite him to stay longer. Maybe watch a movie. After all, in his experience, women were afraid to be alone, and the circumstances of that murder had made things even more frightening.

But Valentina clearly wasn't just any woman. She simply said, "Thank you."

"Well, I guess I've bothered you enough for today, and it looks like it's not raining anymore, so I'll be on my way."

He hesitated, giving her plenty of time to tell him she wanted him to stay. But she simply nodded and walked him to the door.

"Thank you so much for dinner. The rumors are true. You really are an amazing cook.”

She gave him a shy smile and once he was out of her house, she waved goodbye before closing the door.

Wyatt drove home, his head down. *Shit.* Yes, he’d gotten most of what he’d wanted from Valentina. But for some reason, he couldn’t feel elated by that. Probably because he’d wanted some dessert with his dinner. Melissa had been two days ago, and he usually didn’t go that long between women.

The moment he got home, Wyatt grabbed his phone to check on Valentina’s texts, but she wasn’t texting anybody at that moment so he put it down. For a while at least he tried his best to relax on the couch and to convince himself that everything was going to be all right, that he had the situation under control.

Yeah, that’s what you thought when you came here, wasn’t it? he said to himself, but he shook his head, refusing to listen to those thoughts which would only make things worse.

Instead, he turned on the TV to see if there was anything interesting on Netflix.

Yes, he repeated to himself. *Everything is under control. It will be all right.*

Twelve

It was a pretty summer's day, hot but with a clear blue sky and the scent of flowers in the air. That morning, Valentina had decided to go for a walk with Dante and Luna before lunch so she could enjoy the weather and stretch her legs some.

The dogs cavorted happily in front of her, playing with each other or barking at the deer that every so often were brave enough to take a shy peek through the thickness of the forest. As she meandered down the road, Valentina thought about her recent conversation with Jack.

He'd seemed so upset about his boss sending someone from headquarters to help him, and it wasn't like him. Normally, he let things like that roll off his back.

She understood why he was upset as no man liked to be told his business, although she personally thought it wasn't that big of a deal. If the case was that hard, maybe having somebody by his side would help him to get back to her faster. She liked that idea. She couldn't deny that she missed him.

But she got the feeling that he wasn't going to take it so easily. That meant he was probably under stress.

She'd thought about telling him that, that maybe a few days' rest would do him good, but she didn't want to add to it. And if he decided to take off from work after failing to reconcile that case, he'd probably be miserable to deal with.

Her stomach distracted her from those thoughts with a loud

growl. Clasping her hands over it, she decided to head back home to eat lunch. She and the dogs slowly walked back the way they came, all three of them dragging from the heat that was becoming more and more intense as noon approached.

Once she was in front of her house, Valentina stopped to check the mail. Suddenly, Dante and Luna barked. She lifted her head up, shielding her eyes from the sun with her free hand, noticing a man approaching her on the road with a slow, precise waddle. *What on earth?*

"I'm so sorry to bother you, ma'am," the man said, short of breath, taking off his strange and old brimmed hat to greet her with a wide and kind smile. He bowed in a chivalrous manner, showing off the thinning spot on the top of his head. "But I just moved in to the house next to yours and I thought that it would have been rather rude of me not to introduce myself. My name is John J. Watson, at your service."

Valentina was baffled. What a bizarre character. He looked like he came from another time: he was maybe in his sixties, kind of chubby, quite overdressed for their corner of the woods, with a thick British accent. And that old-fashioned hat! She couldn't help but smile.

"Oh, I heard that I was getting a neighbor in. My name's Valentina," she replied. "Valentina Bianco. It's nice to meet you."

"Valentina. You are not from around here, either?"

"That's right. I'm from Milan, Italy. But I've been here for a few years."

"Italy! Very good, very good. It is a pleasure to meet you as well," the man said, putting the hat back on his head. "I hope this doesn't seem inappropriate, but it would be an honor to have you to dinner tomorrow at my new house to get acquainted, as good neighbors always should do. You can tell me all about this place I'm calling home for the time being."

She smiled, slightly taken aback by the invitation. Considering that she lived in the middle of nowhere, it was ironic that both an actor from L.A. and now this odd British guy were now living so close, and both wanted to get to know her. What were the chances?

And will Jack be jealous about it?

But he was unassuming and gentle, with overly formal manners, like a kind, old uncle. She didn't want to be rude and decline. But then again, she'd sensed that Jack had been a little upset about Wyatt. "Well, ordinarily, I'd love to, but—"

"Bring your husband, and your kids, if you—"

She was already shaking her head.

"Or a friend, if you'd like!" he said with a grin. "The more, the merrier. I'd love to meet more of the town's residents. My door is always open to people. As they say, a stranger is just a friend you haven't met yet!"

Valentina had to restrain herself from laughing. Was she that transparent? "Oh, then in that case, I'd love to. I don't have a husband, but I'd love to bring my friend, Michelle. She lives right in that house, down the way." She pointed.

His big blue eyes, as kind as his smile, brightened up when she said that and his smile, if possible, became even wider. "Brilliant!"

He was handsome for an older gentleman. Who knew? He might be right up Michelle's alley. Michelle was in her sixties and had been single for as long as Valentina had known her. She always managed just fine, alone, but every once in a while, Valentina got the impression that she was lonely. Maybe it could be a love match? She couldn't help smiling at the thought.

"I could bring some wine if you'd like," she offered.

"How kind of you! Some red wine would actually be splendid!"

"Red wine it is, then."

Watson smiled at her again. "Very well then," he said, removing a piece of invisible lint from his worn jacket. "I simply cannot wait! Dinner will be ready by seven. But please do come as early as you like. I don't mind the company in the least."

And with that, he took his hat off once again and said goodbye to her, then slowly strolled away with that funny waddle of his. He reminded her a bit of a penguin. For a moment, she couldn't help but stare at him, still puzzled by the unexpected encounter.

Later that day, as Valentina was making some tea for herself, she called Michelle to invite her to Watson's dinner.

"Oh, Lola told me that another new *invader* was coming. From the way she spoke about him, I thought he was from Mars. An Englishman, you say?" Michelle said after Valentina told her about the new member of their community. "I can't believe how our street, in the middle of nowhere, is so multicultural! And here I was thinking I'd have to fly to Europe to experience this kind of culture."

"So you'll come?"

"Hmm, well, Valentina, I have to check my busy social schedule." She let out a laugh. "Of course, I'd love to come with you."

"That's awesome!" Valentina exclaimed, pouring the tea and smelling the sweet essence of the honey she'd just added to it. "He invited us for tomorrow night at seven, but we can go earlier, if you want. So if you stop over here at six-thirty, we can walk over together."

"I can't wait to meet this gentleman," she replied with a giggle. "He really sounds like a fascinating person."

"He definitely is, trust me. And you're right—I can't believe all the interesting residents we're getting here at Long Lakes. Maybe next time, we *will* have someone from Mars."

Michelle laughed. "Should I bring something? Maybe a dessert?"

"Oh, yes! Good idea!" Valentina sat down on her couch, enjoying the air conditioning which, with its subtle humming, was offering her some relief from the dry hotness of the afternoon. "I'm sure that he would love to try one of your pies."

"I'll bring that, then! Black bottom?"

"Oh, yes. No one can resist your Black bottom pie," Valentina said, already tasting the rum-sweetened cream and chocolate on her tongue.

The two of them went on chatting, and their conversation ended up once again on the recent murder that the police were still investigating. Though articles about the horrific crime were still featured on the website where Valentina got her news, it was no longer a top headline. That meant they had no new information.

"The more time that goes on, the more unsettled I get," Michelle said.

"Why is that?" Valentina asked.

"Because, think about it. If it's a serial killer, he probably wouldn't strike while the police are on high alert. He'd wait until the media and police attention has simmered down. When residents have let their guard down, and least expect it."

Valentina nodded. That made sense. A shiver ran down the length of her spine. "Did Lola tell you about those sightings? In the woods?"

"Yes. It's creepy. Probably just animals or hunters or whatnot, but you never can be too careful. I signed that petition to get more guards on staff. I think we need them, so if it increases our homeowner's association fees, I'm all for it."

"Yes, me too. Better to be safe than sorry."

"Well, I think a nice dinner will help distract us from those grim thoughts," Michelle finally said.

Valentina said, "Yes. I think it will. And I do think it will be a pleasant evening."

After Valentina hung up, she realized she had a text from Bea. *Matt and I are going to Miami this weekend to check out the college scene there!*

She frowned. The last thing she wanted to think of was Bea and her boyfriend going away together to a strange town. It was enough that Bea was a couple hundred miles away now, at her school in Nashville. She barely got to see her now as it was. But if she was in Miami, even farther away, would she *ever* see her?

But her daughter was an adult now. Valentina could give her opinion, but she couldn't forbid Bea from making her own choices. Besides, Bea never took to being told what to do. Antonio was the one who ruled their house with an iron fist, and it was probably that reason why, when they split up, Bea had decided to stay in America with Valentina.

So she typed back, *Stay safe, tesoro.*

She went back to work while finishing her tea, and gradually darkness descended. She thought about what Lola had said about strange people, peeking in windows, and wished she had blinds over all of hers.

When night had come fully, she turned on all the lights in the house, and thought about calling Jack for the company. She would have loved to tell Jack about that new neighbor of hers, but he was probably too busy and stressed with his case, so she decided not to disturb him.

That night, she tried to keep her thoughts on the thrill of the upcoming dinner engagement, and just what wine she should bring to impress her new friend. *Watson's name and appearance are so interesting,* she told herself. *I can't wait to see his house. I wonder if he has a study with floor–to-ceiling bookcases, and if he smokes a pipe by a giant crackling fireplace? Maybe his house is adorned with coats of arms and suits of armor?*

She laughed to herself at the thought, but almost instantly after that her mind trailed to what might, or might not be, outside the windows, peeking in at her.

Thirteen

The evening after Valentina first met Watson, she stood in front of her mirror, checking her outfit. She was wearing a modest blouse, belted over a long, flowing flowered skirt—which was as dressed up as she usually got.

Not too long after she finished putting in her hoop earrings, she heard a knock at the door. Michelle, right on time as usual. She rushed to it, hugging her friend.

"You look beautiful!" Michelle said when she stepped back. "Do you think I'm underdressed?"

Michelle was wearing jeans and a sweater, which was what she always wore. No make-up. Valentina had hoped she'd put a little more care into her appearance, since she was meeting an eligible gentleman. But maybe Michelle had been alone so long she'd forgotten what it was like to try to get the opposite sex to notice her.

Even so, she didn't want to make Michelle feel out of place.

"Oh, no. You're not. As far as I know, there's no dress code for this event!" Valentina said with a wink, grabbing her wine and heading through the front door. She blew kisses to Dante and Luna, pulled the door shut, and linked an arm through Michelle's. "Let us be off."

As the two of them walked toward Watson's house, Valentina couldn't help noticing something was bothering her friend. "Is everything all right?"

Michelle pressed her lips together, then stopped and looked over her shoulder at her house. "It's nothing, really. Just… I actually almost cancelled on you. Mina's not feeling too well. I had her at the vet earlier today."

"Oh, no, really?"

She nodded. "Taylor's over there with her now, because I didn't want to leave her alone. She needs constant attention."

"I understand."

"The vet said she'd be fine, but you know me. Mina's the only family I have left." She pouted.

"No, of course." She rubbed her friend's shoulder. "If you want to go back—"

"No, no." A smile spread across her face. "That would be rude. Besides, I'm sure he's already waiting for us. I'll stay an hour at most. That's all."

Valentina nodded. It sounded like a good escape plan in case Mr. Watson wound up being not just pleasantly odd, but a real creep. "Of course."

They began to walk again toward their host's cabin, which was hidden by overgrown trees and brush.

"I can't believe I didn't even realize that somebody moved into this house," Valentina said to Michelle as they reached the long gravel driveway to the building.

"I hadn't noticed either, to be honest. The place is so buried by vegetation. I wonder what brought him here."

"I'm sure that we'll find out soon enough."

They were now at the end of the driveway in front of the large cabin. Michelle quickly fixed her hair.

"How do I look?" she asked Valentina while a pleasant breeze blew through the tree branches, making the night air cooler.

"Amazing, as always."

They smiled at each other and then Valentina knocked at the door. A couple of seconds later, Watson opened it, immediately greeting them, and Valentina proceeded to introduce him to Michelle.

"I am so glad that you decided to accept my invitation," he said, gently grabbing Michelle's hand to kiss it. Michelle looked as puzzled as Valentina did the day before, blushing when Watson pressed his lips against her knuckles in a gentlemanly fashion. "Oh, pie?"

She handed it to him. "It's my black bottom pie."

"It's the best pie in the state," Valentina offered. "And I brought red, as you desired. A slightly aged Chianti."

"Wonderful! Please, come in." He took the pie and wine and guided them inside, where the mouth-watering smell of chicken and potatoes made everything even more inviting.

"Your house looks so nice, Mr. Watson," Michelle said, looking around.

"Oh, well, thank you. And please, call me John."

Michelle smiled as her eyes kept darting in every direction. Valentina had to agree with her: the house was beautiful and the furniture even more so, even if everything looked pretty old. Well, maybe what looked old to her was considered "antique" by some. She was no expert.

However, although the furniture was nice, it looked like the house of a single, frugal, modest man. She was expecting something way more eccentric, but maybe she'd just gotten the wrong impression of John.

"Dinner will be ready soon," John said. "In the meantime, it would be my pleasure to show you something, if you'll just come this way."

Valentina and Michelle exchanged a curious glance before following the man to a set of narrow stairs that brought them downstairs from the kitchen. Once they were down in the basement, Valentina found all the eccentricity that she was looking for.

"This is my little passion project," John explained, as his guests stared at it in pure wonder. "I arranged it so that it would look like the original Baker Street from Arthur Conan Doyle's masterpieces. Are you familiar with his work?"

"Who isn't?" Michelle said, still looking around.

"I am his biggest fan," John went on with pride. "And I will not lie to you, I am actually a detective myself."

Valentina was barely able to pay attention to what he was saying, still admiring the basement. He did not lie; it was clear he'd taken great pains to make the room look exactly like the famed brownstone on Baker Street. The basement's door had a plate on it that said 221B, with small gas lamps from the eighteen hundreds surrounding it. But inside was the real beauty: it looked exactly like Sherlock Holmes's apartment, with the worn wingback chairs, the massive fireplace, the dark red tapestries, the orange carpet, the bookshelves and even a set of heavy curtains that partially covered a false window. The bookshelves contained the entire series of Conan Doyle's books and on the surfaces were all kinds of gadgets related to Sherlock Holmes and his adventures. Stepping in there felt like going back in time.

"Oh, my," Valentina exclaimed. "I thought you were just renting this place."

"I am, I am, indeed," he said with pride. "The furniture upstairs came with the house, but I found it rather dull. Not my style. So I had my own things sent to me. I do plan on staying here for quite a while. Wherever I travel, I try not to pick up and leave until I've fully immersed myself in a place."

Michelle gazed at him with admiration. "How wonderful." Was it just Valentina, or was there a spark in her eyes?

John went on explaining to them how Conan Doyle's work had inspired him since he was very young, how Sherlock Holmes's books were his absolute favorites and how he always felt that—especially because of his name—he was somehow destined to become a famous detective.

"My career allowed me to live all kinds of adventures," John said, before he was interrupted by the arrival of a large black cat with long fur, huge yellow eyes and a long tail that he elegantly swung back and forward.

"Oh my, Sherlock, you arrive just in time!" John said, grabbing the cat, which purred loudly against his chest.

"What a beautiful cat you have, John!" Michelle exclaimed, cautiously putting a hand forward to pet him.

"Thank you! This is my faithful partner, Sherlock. He actually helped me to solve a few rather complicated cases."

Valentina could not believe what she was seeing. She was so amused by all of it that she wished she could grab her phone right there to take pictures of the basement to send to Jack and her daughter.

The three of them went back upstairs and sat at the modest dining room table, where John served them chicken, potatoes and other delicious-looking vegetables that were all perfectly cooked. In the meantime, Sherlock curled up on the red recliner in the living room and started to snore loudly.

As they ate dinner, Michelle kept asking John about his adventures and the places he visited. As it turned out, Watson did travel quite a lot, all over the world, until he ended up in Cincinnati, Ohio with his wife, until she unfortunately passed away five years ago.

Tired of living in the city on his own, with not many friends to leave behind, John decided to find a rural place with more suitable weather, and the place he found was Long Lakes.

"As soon as I found this community online," John said, cutting up a piece of chicken, "I fell in love with it. I grew up in the countryside, in Cornwall, you see? The city is no place for me. I love peace and quiet. City people are always in such a rush!"

Valentina noticed how captivated Michelle was by the man's words. A couple of times during the dinner, she almost felt like a third wheel. John and her friend had clearly clicked since the beginning. It was nice to see Michelle with such a bright smile on her face; she hadn't seen her smile that much since before she learned her son Rob had been struggling with rehab.

They ate Michelle's delicious pie, sitting on the chairs in the basement, surrounded by the magic of Baker Street, while the many books curiously observed them from the shelves.

John even shared some brandy with them. Valentina usually didn't drink anything besides wine, but the older man was so polite that it was impossible to say no to him. It was too strong for her taste, but she sipped it slowly, pretending to like it.

"It's very nice that you have this cave down here," Michelle remarked. "No windows. So you can avoid the creeper."

John stared blankly. "Creeper?"

Valentina nodded. "I don't want to turn you against this place, but I'm sure you heard of the murder that happened outside the development?"

His face fell. "I did indeed. Sad stuff."

"Yes. Well, there have been all these sightings of people snooping about the development, supposedly, peering in windows. It's got the people around here a little nervous."

"I see. I can imagine," he said, shaking his head. "Have either of you seen this creeping fellow?"

They both shook their heads. Michelle said, "People around here are fond of spreading rumors and tall tales. So it might be nothing. Even so, it's important that we all look out for each other. As neighbors."

He poured another glass of brandy and nodded. "Most certainly. I will keep my eye out."

Sometime later, after a lot of laughter and an extremely pleasant evening, Valentina yawned and checked the time on the old grandfather clock.

"Oh, goodness!" she said with surprise. "It's after ten! Michelle, didn't you say you needed to be back for Mina?"

Michelle blinked. "Oh! Poor Taylor. She's probably wondering where I am!" She checked her phone. "No messages, at least."

Valentina sighed with relief.

"Mina is *my* cat," Michelle explained to John. "She was a bit under the weather tonight, so I had a pet sitter watch her. Which reminds me, if you need one for Sherlock, I can refer her to you. Her name's Taylor."

"Brilliant!" he said, stroking his cat as he led them upstairs.

"I had such a great time, John. Thank you so much for inviting us," Michelle said.

"It's true," Valentina added. "Thank you for the lovely time and the amazing food."

John blushed slightly. "Made even better by the wonderful pie and the wine," he added. "Thank you for keeping this old man company so exquisitely. I hope we will have more chances to chat."

When they had gone halfway down the driveway, Valentina turned around to find him still passionately waving at them.

"It is late. Too late. Poor old Mina. But I had so much fun!" Michelle repeated to Valentina once they were out of Watson's sight.

"I'm glad. I had fun myself. And I'm sure Mina is fine. Taylor could've just come over here if there was a problem."

"True," Michelle said with a nod. "It's incredible what he did with that basement. And all the places he visited! He's such an interesting man. And that accent! Oh, it's irresistible!"

Valentina smiled, keeping to herself the fact that Michelle sounded like she was getting a crush on him. They walked together for a little bit before saying goodnight to each other. It was after ten by the time she got into her bedroom to change into her pajamas. As she climbed into bed, she checked her phone one last time. There was a text from Jack: *Sorry I've been MIA all day. Busy. Have a good night.*

That didn't sound good. It sounded like more of the same stress he'd been having all week.

She replied to Jack's goodnight text with a, *Sorry! I've been out. Hope you have a good night as well.*

She'd tell him everything about her special evening later. With all the stress he was under, he probably wouldn't be interested, anyway.

She lay down, listening to the coyotes and the owls, and found herself drifting, still thinking about 221B Baker Street. It was only in the few seconds before she closed her eyes and sleep took her away that her mind went to the Long Lakes creeper, she tilted her head toward the window, and—in the darkness beyond her windowpane—she could've sworn she saw a human figure, peering at her.

Fourteen

My guardian demon is out in full force tonight.

There is trouble on the horizon, and I don't like it. My guardian demon doesn't either. I can feel it inside, moving, growing restless. It does not like this one bit.

And when it gets like that, watch out.

Sitting here, in my hiding spot, I see it all. I see more than anyone in this godforsaken rat hole knows. They think they can outwit me? I am much too smart for them. They think that stupid girl is the end? Oh, no. I will do whatever it takes to get what I want.

And there's only so much time that I can play nice. Watching that Italian bitch and her old biddy friend walk home from that strange little man's house, I grind my teeth, feeling the rage bubbling inside me.

They think they are safe here in this quiet little town where very little happens. They think that they can do what they like, with no consequences whatsoever.

But no one stands in the way of me getting what I want.

No, it won't be long.

Soon, they are all going to pay.

And I'll start with the Italian one. Yes, she thinks she's so smart, but she has no idea what she's up against. I think the guardian demon inside me would like very much to stare into her eyes as they bulge out of her head, to hear her gasp her last breath as she struggles.

Oh yes, the demon will like that very much, indeed.

Fifteen

Jack stared at his suitcase, just as he had been doing periodically for almost the past hour, before grabbing the handle to walk out of his hotel room. As he crossed the long hallway, he wondered for the hundredth time if this was actually a good idea.

Then he went to his phone and looked at the text from Valentina. *Sorry, I've been out.*

It had come through to him at a little before eleven in the evening.

His mind had fired with all sorts of scenarios, very few of them plausible considering Long Lakes wasn't big on night life. In fact, there was hardly anything to do around there once the sun went down. So that meant something was up. Something had changed between them. And the only thing he could think of?

This actor guy…

It certainly hadn't sounded like a good idea to his boss. Picking up and leaving an assignment in the middle of things? There was no doubt that he wasn't in a position to make such a bold move, but Jack knew the guy that was assigned to him and that he was good enough to handle things without him around. Most likely it would be easier for him without Jack in the way.

Still, he had this feeling that he was being overdramatic and too jealous, and that there was a reasonable explanation.

If only he could think of what that could be.

Valentina was going to think that he didn't trust her enough. He couldn't help it, though. When she told him about how eager that actor seemed to be to spend some time with her, and that he'd even invited himself to dinner, in her house, he couldn't think straight anymore. He was useless on this case.

And after that text, on pure impulse, he bought a ticket for the first flight to Nashville so that he could spend some time back at Long Lakes.

Besides, he wasn't doing it simply out of jealousy. No, his instinct told him that there was more to the story. An actor, staying in Long Lakes of all places? Why would a famous actor decide to spend time in a place like that when he probably owned multiple properties on some isolated island or some trendy, upscale corner of the world, far more appealing than the woods of Tennessee?

Something was wrong.

Plus, there had been a murder there. There was nothing wrong with Jack going back to make sure that his girlfriend was safe.

Jack took a cab to the airport and boarded, hoping for a smooth flight so he could catch a little shut-eye on the way. But it was a turbulent one that did little to calm his nerves.

When he finally got to Nashville, after getting his suitcase, he stretched in front of the airport, breathing the air, feeling so much better now that he had solid land under his feet. He spotted his colleague's car and waved as he headed toward it.

"Hey, Jack! Had a good flight?" Louie asked him, opening the trunk for him.

"I don't even want to talk about it!" Jack muttered, lifting his heavy suitcase, feeling sweaty from all the nausea that the turbulence had caused him. He could not wait to jump in the shower, but unfortunately, they still had a long way before getting to Long Lakes.

"That good, huh?"

"Yeah well, I'm sure you heard Dees grumbling around the office, didn't you?" Jack eyed him as he slid into his seat, not sure he wanted to hear the answer to that one.

Louie laughed. "Did I! I'm telling you, it's pretty nice

not to be number one on Dees' shitlist, for once."

A sick feeling settled in Jack's gut. As thankful as he was to have his friend to pick him up at the airport, he wasn't in the mood for any more conversation about work.

Jack took advantage of that time to rest, after chit chatting for a bit with his friend Louie who was so kind to pick him up on one of his rare days off. They talked about Louie's wife and about his kid's big baseball game, then changed the subject to Jack's case but, soon after that, he started to doze off, and, staring at the trees outside, he fell asleep.

It was Louie who woke him up once they were almost at the community's gates, asking him for better directions than the ones offered by the GPS.

"Man, this place is huge, ain't it?" Louie commented while slowly driving on the pothole-filled road inside the gates of the development.

"You have no idea," Jack replied, feeling impatient all of a sudden. He could not wait to see Valentina's face. She'd be surprised; he hadn't told her he was coming.

"Seems beautiful, though. Even if there isn't anything for miles."

Jack nodded. "It can get boring after a while. Turn here."

Louie laughed and made the turn. They drove in front of the general store, the parking lot of which was practically empty as usual. Ellie was probably in there, working the cash register, desperate to chew someone's ear off with the gossip of the day. Then they passed the pool, and the stables. He noticed Lola's car outside the barn—she, like Valentina, kept a horse there. Knowing Lola, she was probably busy boring to death the new stable manager with her own gossip. The previous stable managers had been arrested for drug possession and intent to distribute, and kicked off the property.

Funny, at the start of the year, he hadn't even known where Long Lakes was. Now he actually had a history here. It felt strange to be back here, even though he'd only been gone a few weeks.

They finally arrived in front of Valentina's house. Jack yawned and stretched his arms over his head, feeling his eyes droop, even though he was excited to see her. Once he got his suitcase from the trunk, he thanked Louie for the ride and shook his hand.

"I owe you one. Big time. Want to come in?"

"No, I'm sure you two want some alone-time." He winked.

He sure hoped Valentina did, and that she hadn't been eyeing up any movie stars, instead. "You know how to get back to the main gate?" he asked him.

"I think I can manage," he said. "Tell Val I said hello."

And with that, he jumped back in his car, made a quick K-turn in the drive, and drove off, spreading a large cloud of dust in the air as he sped away.

Jack went immediately up to the door and knocked a couple of times. He could ear Dante and Luna barking from the inside, but Valentina didn't seem to be home, so he reached in his backpack and got out his own key, something Valentina had minted for him a few weeks after the incident with the drug ring.

"Valentina?" he called as he walked inside while the dogs happily jumped on him, licking

his hands and begging to be petted. "I missed you too, guys. Say, your beautiful owner isn't here, is she?"

The dogs kept wagging their tails, looking at him with their big, soft brown eyes.

"Thanks for your help," he said with a sigh, walking around the house. He looked out at the garden, and the lake, then over toward Michelle's house, seeing no sign of her. Then he went upstairs and confirmed the place was empty.

She was probably out riding Sunny, or pedaling her bike around the development. It was a beautiful day, and Valentina never sat still for long.

Still, he couldn't help the feeling of disappointment that came over him. He'd been hoping for a vibrant Welcome Home from the moment he'd stepped out of the hotel. He knew it was his own fault for not telling her he was coming, but he'd really wanted to see her face.

Or maybe he'd just wanted to catch her in the act.

No, that wasn't the case. He'd caught Yvonne in the middle of a lot of lies, and it wasn't any fun. If Valentina was lying to him, a large part of him would rather have not known.

Heaving another disappointed sigh, he decided to take a shower in the meantime. He went upstairs, stripped, and ran the water. He let out a grunt of relief the moment the warm water hit his body and he felt his tense muscles finally relaxing. Then he grabbed some lounge pants and a T-shirt from the dresser, changed, and went down to grab a beer.

Just as he was getting downstairs, he heard the door's knob turn and he started smiling even before he saw her. As soon as Valentina walked inside, her expression turned from extremely confused—and maybe a little scared?—to happy.

She patted her chest and let out a gasp. "Oh. I thought you were an intruder!" she said with a smile. "Thank goodness it's you, Jack! I am so happy you're here!"

He opened his arms, glad to finally have that genuine welcome. She bridged the distance and hugged him tight, and all of his worries about her somehow falling in love with a mysterious movie star suddenly seemed silly. He held her tight, feeling even more of the stress fade away.

"What are you doing here?" she asked with a smile, her arms still around his neck as she peered up at him.

"Surprise!"

She stood on her toes and kissed him. "You mean… the case is over?"

Some of the stress edged back. He didn't want to think of work. "Not exactly. But I missed you, and the guy they assigned me can handle the job without me for a few days."

"Well, that's great news. I'm so happy you're here."

"Me too."

She let him go and frantically started looking in the fridge before getting out a bottle of wine.

"We have to celebrate," she said, taking out a couple of glasses.

Jack walked up behind her as she fussed in the kitchen, hugging her tight as she carefully poured the wine in the glasses. He rested his head on her shoulder and smelled her perfume, finally feeling at home. "So… where were you coming from? You smell like fresh air."

She laughed. "Oh. I was just delivering a casserole to a new neighbor. I feel bad for him, being all alone in his house. So I was just being neighborly."

The movie star. He fought the urge to make more of it than it was. Valentina loved to cook, and was always generous with her food. "What did he get out of you?"

She giggled as he tickled her side. "What do you mean?"

"If it was that special *ciambotta* you make, I'll be jealous."

"It was not. It was just a regular old lasagna."

"Oh," he groaned, clutching his heart. "You got me right where it hurts."

She laughed and handed him his wine. "Would you like me to make a meal? You must be starving."

His gaze darkened as he looked at her. He took both their glasses and set them down. "Actually, I have an appetite for something else, instead," he said, ducking his head and kissing her neck.

That night, after a very passionate couple of hours to celebrate their reunion, Jack forced himself to leave Valentina's warm and soft body and quietly went downstairs. He needed to check something before tackling the unpleasant task of discussing the actor with Valentina. He wanted solid data to prove that the guy was up to no good. His instinct rarely failed him, and this time it was practically screaming at him. His instinct, or maybe just his jealousy; he didn't know, and he didn't particularly care.

He turned on his laptop and started with a very basic search on the actor's biography. It didn't take him long to find out that Wyatt Rogers was Nashville born and raised, and that he'd even gotten a degree in computer science at the University of Tennessee. That piece of information made all his internal alarms go off. With that kind of degree, the guy was probably not only handsome and rich, but probably pretty smart and tech-savvy.

Meaning, he was a threat.

The more he scrolled, the more his desire to ask Valentina the all-important question intensified.

But it could wait until next morning. Feeling somewhat reassured that he did have good evidence to support his case with Valentina, he joined her back in bed and promptly fell asleep.

The next morning, Valentina suggested having breakfast at the general store. He was still exhausted from the trip and his late-night search, and didn't necessarily want to interact with anybody, but she seemed in a cheerful mood now that he was back and he didn't feel like raining on her parade.

Of course, as soon as they got inside the place, Ellie cornered him. "Hey, there, stranger!" she called, waving. "I didn't know you were back! When did you get in?"

"Last night," he said, offering a smile as he nudged Valentina toward the tables. Maybe she'd get the hint and leave him alone.

That was wishful thinking. She said, "I heard you were in the middle of a big case? In Memphis?"

"That's right. Just taking a few days off to visit my girl." He winked at Valentina.

"Oh, she must be so glad to see you!" she said, her expression turning serious. "I'm sure she told you all about the horrible murder. In fact, we're all glad to have a big, strong man like you around. It's pretty creepy, what's been going—"

"Ellie," Valentina interrupted her. "Jack is pretty tired with all the crimes he's been dealing with. We're just here to have some breakfast and not to talk about any more business."

"Of course. I'm sorry," Ellie said, handing them two menus and motioning to the dining area in the corner of the store. "You guys go sit down, I'll get your orders in a second."

They sat down and looked at the menus, holding hands on the

table like a couple of teenagers who'd just gotten together and couldn't avoid physical contact. Despite the reasons why he came back, and despite Ellie mentioning the murder, Jack felt happy in that moment, so content and yet so needed. When Ellie came, he ordered the ham and cheese omelet, and it was only then that he realized just how hungry he was.

They were finishing breakfast when Michelle entered the store. She was with two people that Jack didn't remember seeing before. One of them was clearly the bizarre British character Valentina recently told him about. It was clear simply because of his extravagant clothes—who wore a formal blazer with cravat in this heat, in Long Lakes?

"Michelle!" Valentina said, waving at her friend, who immediately smiled and approached their table with the two strangers.

"Jack! You're back," Michelle exclaimed as soon as she was closer. Michelle had once been a little standoffish to him because of an earlier investigation, when he believed her to be a suspect in the drug ring, but their past frictions had been put aside, and now they got along perfectly.

"I am, yes," he replied, taking a sip of his coffee, "I needed a break from my damn case. It's good to be back here."

"It's understandable. Valentina said it was a dog! Oh, I need to introduce you to someone." She turned toward the man. "John, this is Jack, Valentina's boyfriend. Jack, this is John Watson, our new neighbor."

The man took his hat off with a serious expression on his wrinkled, ruddy face. He had thick white hair, a little lighter on top. "At your service," he said with a strong English accent.

Jack nodded at him, repressing the urge to chuckle in front of such a peculiar character. When Valentina had described John Watson to him, he'd thought she was exaggerating. But clearly, she wasn't. He truly did look like he came from another place, another time.

"And this is our new pet sitter, Taylor. Valentina, you remember Taylor?"

Valentina nodded as the young girl shook Jack's hand.

"John and I are actually going to leave both of our cats to her care soon. We… uhm… we decided to take a short trip together."

"Oh?" Valentina blurted.

Michelle blushed. "Yes. We just came in to show Taylor around."

Valentina and Jack looked at each other, sharing a smile. Valentina had mentioned that her friend and her strange neighbor seemed to get along very well from the very first dinner that they had together. She'd wondered whether it meant good things were on the horizon for the two of them, and once again, she was right.

"Where are you guys going?" she asked them, squeezing Jack's hand.

"Oh, we were thinking about the Smokey Mountains. It's so peaceful there."

As if it isn't peaceful enough here, Jack thought.

"Sherlock barely needs a pet sitter," John intervened. "He's so intelligent, he could take care of himself! But Michelle convinced me to let Miss Taylor here take care of him, just in case something happens. And what with all the intrigue around here…"

"Sherlock is John's cat," Michelle explained, smiling at Jack's confused expression.

"Oh, yeah. Makes sense," he said. "And when you say intrigue, you mean… the murder?"

"Not just that. There have been all these weird sightings. People in windows. Figures sneaking in the dark," Michelle explained with a shudder, and John promptly moved to her side to wrap a comforting arm around her.

"There, there, Love," he said, squeezing her. She blushed.

Jack laughed to himself. He wasn't very close with Michelle, but he'd never seen her this way. She looked at least ten years younger.

Good, he thought. *Valentina always said she worried about Michelle being lonely. Now she doesn't have to concern herself with that anymore.*

The group chatted with them for a bit longer before heading

back outside to sit at one of the long tables while he and Valentina finished eating.

"You weren't kidding about that Watson guy," he said once they'd gotten into her car.

"I told you!"

They laughed, and since she was in a good mood, he decided that it was time to have the discussion that he'd been rehearsing in his head for a couple of days now, ever since he decided to come back to Long Lakes. He didn't want to risk turning things sour, but this was important.

"Can I ask you something, Val?"

"Of course! What is it?" she said, still looking in front her as they drove back to her place.

"About your dinner with that actor."

"Oh. You mean Wyatt? What about it? Are you jealous?" she teased him.

He laughed, but even his laugh sounded nervous. He was trying too hard not to let it show. Maybe it was too late for that, anyway. Smart as she was, maybe she'd already figured out why he'd really come back.

His tone turned sober. "Actually, it's a little more serious than that. I'm worried. I really don't understand what this guy is doing here and what he wants from you."

She rolled her eyes before quickly turning to him, giving him one of her amazing smiles.

"What do you mean, what does he want? First he wanted to learn how to kayak. Second, he wanted to try some of my food." She shook her head. "Poor man. I think he might be lonely. We're not as exciting as his Hollywood friends, I'm sure."

Her tone was still light, and it troubled him. Did she need him to spell it out for her? "He's new to this area. There's a murder that just occurred not far from here. Put two and two together, and—"

"What?" She gaped at him. "You're saying Wyatt's a criminal?"

"Well—"

"Jack." She shook her head. "He's a very successful movie star.

Not some psychopath. He has no reason to go around murdering women."

Jack pressed his lips together. From what he'd heard, most of Hollywood was pretty damn crazy.

"You're worrying too much," she said, exactly as he'd expected her to.

"Am I, though?"

"Yes, Jack, you are. He just needed some peace and quiet. I can't think of a better place than this for something like that."

"I can," he said, maybe too harshly, making her frown.

"What's that supposed to mean?"

"I mean, he's filthy rich. Probably has a place in every corner of the world. There are so many different places where he could have gone," he explained, trying to calm his tone down, "somewhere he's got some type of property. Why did he come here, spending money to rent a place out here in the middle of the sticks? And why did he want to hang out with you so badly?"

Her jaw hung open. "Oh my God, you ARE jealous!"

She started laughing. It kind of hurt that she was making fun of him instead of listening. Wasn't that the first thing a cheater did—try to convince their partner that they were crazy? It made him wonder if she was already siding with this guy because she had a crush on him. Or worse. What if they were already sleeping together?

No. No, that wasn't possible.

"Valentina, I'm serious."

She must have heard it his voice because she stopped laughing. She reached for his hand over the console and stroked it.

"Why are you so worried, *amore*?" she said in a low, soothing voice. "I do not know why he chose this place over Hawaii. But he did. Maybe, everywhere he has homes, the paparazzi knows how to find him. Here, it's more secluded. Unexpected. And as to why he sought me out, maybe he was bored out of his mind and just needed some company, that's it. I'm sorry if my hanging out with him made you upset. If you want me not to anymore, then fine. I will make an excuse next time, not to see him."

Now he felt bad, like a stupid jealous boy. But he could feel in his gut that something was wrong. After all, he was a red-blooded man, too. He knew how men thought, how they operated. This Wyatt Rogers wanted something more than innocent company from her. He was sure of it. He wouldn't tell her that, though. Not until he had his proof.

So he said, "I don't want you to do that. But I just care about you, Val. I just don't want you to get hurt."

She pulled back and placed her hand on the steering wheel, gripping it tightly. "So is that why you came back?"

He grabbed the hand back, and squeezed it. "I came back because I missed you and because I want to make sure that you're safe."

"I *am* safe, Jack." She shook her head. "And if you're trying to keep me safe from Wyatt, I assure you, there's no need. He's harmless."

I don't know about that, Jack thought.

"As for the other things, the creepy sightings and whatnot—yes, they're concerning. But I'm an adult. I can take care of myself," she continued.

He nodded. "I know that you can take care of yourself but I wanted to be closer to you, just in case your Italian fire wasn't enough," he joked, and she laughed, making him relax a bit.

They hit a hole in the ground and he grabbed the door's handle. He certainly had not missed these roads.

"Did he happen to be alone at some point? With access to… I don't know… Your purse, or your phone?"

She frowned. "Jack!"

"I know, I know. But humor me."

"No… I don't think so… but why does it matter?"

"He might have touched something that he shouldn't have."

"For what purpose? You just said he's filthy rich. You think he'd pick my pockets, too?"

Now she seemed amused by his theories. He could tell that she understood that he was being very serious but at the same time she didn't seem to completely understand why. She probably thought that he was being paranoid.

"He might have wanted information on you. To access your personal data and do something with it."

She shook her head as she turned to the road that led to her house. "I really don't see why he would do that."

"Look. I've seen weirder things happen. I'm in fraud. This is what I do."

"But why would he do it to *me*?"

"I'm not saying he did. But on the off-chance, I should probably look into it."

"I took a quick shower while he was there," she finally admitted, "It had just rained and I was soaked. I can't remember, but I guess that I could have left my phone on the counter while I was showering."

That was it. He was probably thinking he could skim off her account. Rich or not, didn't matter. He'd seen all types of thieves. Maybe Wyatt had a problem. He'd studied IT, after all. Maybe he liked to do things simply because he knew he couldn't get caught. "I'll need to see your phone then."

Her tone turned wooden. "If you must."

He ignored her comment and tried his best to not let her skepticism get on his nerves. After what had happened with that drug dealer, he couldn't understand how she could take his suspicions so lightly.

They went inside without another word.

"After this," she said, handing him the device, "will you promise you'll try to relax and enjoy the rest of the day with me?"

He sighed. He hadn't wanted to put a damper on things, but even so… the mood was decidedly less jovial. "I promise."

He went through her phone but couldn't find anything. Then he asked her to check her own bank accounts, but she didn't notice anything unusual. Still, as he stared at the screen, he felt like he was missing something. He wasn't the right person to do this.

"I need to bring this to Nashville tomorrow," he told her.

Both of her eyebrows shot up. "But Jack… you just got here."

"It will take the guys there no more than one day, I promise. I just want to make sure that he didn't install anything."

"Install something? Why? He's an actor, Jack, not a hacker."

You have no idea, he thought, but decided not to press it any further.

"Just for tomorrow."

She rolled her eyes again but agreed to let him do as he wished. He immediately called his office in Nashville and got on the phone with Louie, the resident hacker, explaining the situation. He arranged to bring in the phone the following day.

"Now, can we please go for a walk?" Valentina asked him once he'd ended the call.

"Yes. Let me just change into something more suitable."

She nodded and sat on the couch to wait for him. While he was in her bedroom, changing, he tried to force himself to relax, but instead, he thought about that actor.

You're here with Valentina. Try to enjoy it.

Downstairs, Valentina grabbed his hand, calling the dogs outside, while he couldn't stop thinking about what might be on her phone. He didn't care if she didn't believe him. Her safety came before everything else.

Sixteen

The following morning, Jack and Valentina were having breakfast quietly, sitting on the porch. The night before, after he told her that he wanted to get her phone to the FBI, things got a little tense between them. Valentina was reluctant and skeptical, while he felt frustrated because she didn't believe him.

And maybe he was overreacting. But after what had happened to her before, he thought for sure that she'd see his way. After all, Valentina had never expected that her neighbors in Long Lakes could be criminals.

He wasn't overreacting. He was being cautious.

Of course, if she knew the whole of it…

He didn't want to tell her that he'd been researching Wyatt, because the last thing he needed was for her to think he was stalking the guy. He needed more proof before he could tell her about that.

"Are you sure you still want to do this?" Valentina asked him while she stirred the sugar in her coffee.

"We already talked about this," he said with a resolute light in his blue eyes.

She didn't say anything else and went on eating her breakfast. In other circumstances, he would have felt hurt, but right now was not the moment to wallow in self-pity. Her safety was what counted the most, and he could not forget that.

Besides, he didn't want to fight anymore now that he was here after such a long time apart.

"You trust me, right?" he asked, grabbing her hand.

"Of course, I do! I just think that sometimes, being a Fed makes you see danger where there is none."

He kissed her hand. Yes, that was true—being surrounding by criminals and fraudsters all the time often made him feel like the world was full of nothing but scammers and cheats. Sure, at first, he'd thought that maybe he was being paranoid, that it was all in his head, but now that he knew about Wyatt's degree in computer science from the University of Tennessee, it didn't sound so crazy after all.

After breakfast, Jack grabbed Valentina's phone and headed outside to his own car.

"I still don't understand why you have to do this," Valentina said once again as Jack hopped into his car. "You just got here. What's the rush?"

"I just want to make sure, Val." He smirked at her. "Besides, Louie told me on the ride over that he's really bored. This'll give him something to do. So he can keep his hand in."

She sighed. She didn't believe him. He had to admit, it was a pretty flimsy excuse. He closed the door, hanging his arm out of the open window.

"I promise that if I don't find anything, I'll just forget about it."

She didn't seem convinced and simply replied with an "Okay," before leaning toward the car to kiss him.

"I think you're wasting your time," she repeated.

He ignored the sting of her comment.

"I know, but it's just a precaution."

Valentina nodded, crossing her arms while he started the car.

Suddenly, something came to him. "Would you—"

She stared at him expectant. "Would I what?"

He shook his head. He'd wanted to ask her not to see Wyatt. But then she'd really think he was a jealous boyfriend. So instead, as he backed down the driveway, he said, "Nothing. Lock your doors and windows. Be safe, okay? There's weird stuff going on."

"Yes, of course."

"I love you."

"I love you too," she waved at him. He took a quick glance at her phone on the passenger seat. He really hoped that he was doing the right thing.

On the one hand, he hoped he was wrong because it would mean that he was probably being paranoid and Valentina was safe, even if he would have looked like the overly jealous type. But on the other hand, if his people in Nashville found something on her phone that meant that Wyatt Rogers really represented a threat, and he would do everything in his power to make sure that he never got close to Valentina again.

His drive to Nashville was a quiet one. Alone in the car, with not even any music in the background, Jack kept thinking about what he had discovered the previous night about that man and about the fact that it seemed pretty irresponsible of Valentina to let him in her house like that.

By the time he arrived at the FBI office, he was more than ready to discover the truth. Louie was waiting for him and, as soon as the two met in the main hallway, Jack handed him the phone.

"Yeah. Like I said. Anything suspicious. If any spyware was put on it, I want to know."

Louie turned it over in his hands. "No problem, Boss. But what are you thinking you might find?"

"She left it alone, and with someone pretty suspicious," he said vaguely. "And some strange things have been happening around her neighborhood."

He raised an eyebrow. "Around there? I thought *nothing* happened around there?"

He smiled. "You know, it's *probably* nothing, at least, I hope it is, but I just want to make sure."

Louie nodded. "Leave it to me."

Jack thanked him and retreated to his desk to wait for the verdict.

Sitting in his desk chair, he tried to go through his email and get some work done. But his legs kept bouncing nervously as he stared at the clock every two seconds, impatient to know what his colleagues were finding. After a while though, it was impossible for him to sit still on that chair, so he got up to get a coffee and maybe something to snack on from the cafeteria. Caffeine was not something he needed right now, but he had to do *something*.

At least the familiar smell of coffee and sandwiches of the cafeteria made him feel at home. That morning, it had been nice to wake up next to Valentina instead of waking up alone in the hotel room. This wasn't Valentina's place, but it sure beat a lonely hotel room.

Leila, the office admin, walked in and smiled broadly at him, clearly happy to see him back.

"Where have you been, Bub?" she asked while he scanned the menu.

"I was working on a case in Memphis," he explained. "Technically, I still am, but there is something that I needed to check."

"I see. Well, good luck with it, Bub." She gnawed on her lip, and finally said, "When are you coming back into the office for good? We all miss you around here. What with your injury, and the case, we feel like we haven't seen you in forever."

He shrugged. "I don't know." Truthfully, he'd been thinking about that more and more. Sometimes he thought that if Valentina asked, he'd give it all up. Ask Dees for a transfer to a field office in the eastern part of the state, or just up and quit entirely. Become a man of leisure or get a consulting job somewhere close to her.

But right now, that felt as far away from possibility as ever.

He grabbed a sandwich, took his cup of hot black coffee and sat at one of the metal tables to eat, more impatient than ever. Luckily, by the time he went back to his desk, Louie was standing there, waiting for him.

"You were right," he told him, and Jack froze.

"I was?"

The man nodded. "There is a spy app on this phone, a pretty sophisticated one too. It took us a while to find it and it allows to access to all kinds of private information, as well as emails and texts. All the data on this phone is compromised."

Jack's fists clenched at the news. He felt a strange sort of vindication. Wait until Valentina found out…

"Should we remove it?" Louie asked him, handing him the report, which he looked through, though he couldn't understand much of it.

"No, leave it for now. I'll take it from here. Thank you so much."

His colleague nodded and went back to his lab. Jack immediately sat at his desk to go through the federal files and data to understand what the hell was going on.

He knew something was up, he knew it! At the same time, he really wished he hadn't been right, because that meant that Valentina was in danger once again. What did Rogers want from her? He had to find out, and quickly.

At his computer he pulled up every single piece information that he could find in the federal database regarding the actor. Some of if it he'd already found out on Google, but some other information was even more eye-opening.

It turned out that Wyatt had been working for a Netflix series in L.A. at the same time a girl working on the crew of the same series was murdered in her apartment. Strangled. Jack bent over his desk, face close to the screen as he read the news that described the murder.

Warning alarms went off everywhere. Was Wyatt Rogers a murderer?

He quickly Googled the murder that happened right next to Long Lakes, his stomach growing more uneasy as he read. A strangulation, by a stranger. The MO was exactly the same. But that wasn't the only similarity between the two cases. Both of the women were young, single, pretty. In both instances, there was no sign of forced entry and, also, both houses where the murders took place had a security system that was deftly bypassed by whoever was responsible for those horrible acts, so that the killer wasn't in any of the cameras' footage. Not only that, they were both strangled with their dog's leash.

With his skills, it couldn't have been hard for Wyatt to hack the cameras and the security systems right before breaking into the two women's houses and brutally killing them.

And now Jack was sure that he had already chosen his next victim: Valentina.

Sure, she wasn't as young as these women, but she was pretty, and single, and…

A cold sweat broke out on Jack's forehead. He could not waste any time. He rushed to his boss's office without knocking. Dees, who was sitting at his desk in the midst of taking a sip from his coffee mug, dribbled coffee down his chin and stared in shock.

"What the hell are you doing here?" he said, wiping his chin. "I thought you were taking some time off?"

"I found out something incredible, sir," Jack said.

Dees had a way of staring even the tallest person down. "What are you talking about? Erikson, you'd better start making sense right now. You're already on my shitlist for walking out on that Memphis case. You know, it's still hanging open. Nothing was found."

Jack couldn't care less about the Memphis case now. He tried his best to calm down and went on explaining to his boss everything that he had just discovered. His words were tumbling upon each other while adrenaline was pumping throughout his entire body.

"We need to arrest him immediately," he concluded.

"Arrest who?"

"Wyatt Rogers."

"Wyatt Rogers… the actor? Are you kidding me?"

"I just told you, he's in Long Lakes for some kind of escape. And I think he's the one who killed those two women. It makes sense."

"Okay, okay, Jack, calm down. Your accusations are very serious."

"I know he's guilty! Everything connects back to him! His degree, his sudden appearance at Long Lakes, the murder after he got there, which is exactly like the murder that happened in L.A., and then the fact that he put a damn spy app on my girlfriend's phone!"

Dees put his coffee down, loosening his tie.

"All right. I can't deny that it is all extremely suspicious. I'll have him taken right now for interrogation but I don't know if you should be intervening in this any further. There might be a conflict of interest here."

"Sir, please. I want to go on with this investigation. As a matter of fact, I meant to ask you to take me off the fraud case in Memphis so that I can focus on this and make sure that my girlfriend is safe."

Worry grew in his chest. He needed to tell Valentina about this right away.

Seventeen

I don't like it. I don't like it one bit. She's getting too close. I cannot allow that. I must protect everything I've been working so hard to obtain.

I must protect my life, my past and my future.

Her boyfriend's a Fed. Doesn't that Italian bitch know that everybody is aware of that fact? That fact makes her dangerous. If I let my focus slip for just a second, he will stick his nose where it doesn't belong. He must be distracted. And what better way to distract him than getting his beloved girlfriend? Killing her, of course, but not too fast. Slowly, letting her realize what's going on, allowing her to exhale her last breath knowing full well that she shouldn't have played with fire.

I should have already ended her. Time is running out. Next time, I will not wait.

I will show up at her house wearing my best, sweetest, most irresistible smile. She knows and likes me, so she will be completely unsuspecting and will let me in. Her stupid dogs also know me by now, so they won't make a peep. As soon as she turns her back on me, I will grab one of the dogs' leashes, and I will get closer, closer, and then I will loop the leash around her neck so swiftly she won't know what hit her. Then I will start pulling, harder and harder.

She will make those funny gurgling sounds they always make. They never fail to amuse me; what little dignity we have in life is completely gone at the moment of death. Then she will go slack in my arms, and I will slowly lower her to the floor. Her tongue will be protruding from her mouth, and that also always makes me giggle; it's almost as if they want to mock me during their last moments.

The dogs will sniff her, of course, wondering what's going on, what kind of new funny game their momma is playing. They won't mind me leaving her there, on the floor, and they won't even realize that her eyes will be veiled and glazed. They'll instead beg me for food, or a pet, since the momma doesn't seem to want to give it to them. Pretty soon though, their instinct will kick in and they will know something is wrong. By then, I will already be gone.

Then, in the safety of my new home, I will start imagining her beloved Fed when he eventually finds her. I will imagine him, desperately hugging her lifeless body, unsuccessful as he tries to revive her. Oh, I must not let that exquisitely soothing image lull me into letting my guard down. Complacency is my worst enemy. Still, the thought is lingering in my mind like a lullaby.

The Fed will be so distraught that he will let any thought into investigation drop. Oh, sure, he will want to look into her murder, to seek revenge, but then the FBI will undoubtedly remove him from the case because it's too personal for him, and the other agents won't have a clue what has happened. They will probably connect this murder to that of the bitch in the other community, but what can they do? They will never find out about me. I will be too careful. My technical expertise is far superior to theirs; I know how to keep them in the dark.

This will teach them to stay away from my life, from what's mine. Mine, and nobody else's.

Eighteen

Jack left Bruce Dees' office, unwisely slamming the door behind him, and then paced in front of his desk, mumbling very unflattering words about his supervisor and his decision.

After all I've done, he doesn't want me to participate.

Part of him understood. He didn't work in homicide, and the local police had to be brought in. There were rules with this sort of thing. Plus, there was a chance of letting his emotions get the better of him, since this was personal. But he was the one who discovered all those connections. He was the one who'd built a big case from nothing.

And yet, he'd been cast aside, like he didn't matter. Like he hadn't provided the key evidence to put this murderer behind bars. When he'd asked if they'd at least keep him apprised, his supervisor had simply said, "You'll be informed on a need-to-know basis," which essentially meant, *You don't need to know. This isn't your investigation, so stay out of it.*

His boss wanted him back in Memphis, and because Jack felt sure that an arrest was forthcoming, there was nothing more he could do. Dees had also made it pretty clear that he was tired of seeing Jack not focusing on the cases he was assigned to. Since he was obviously still working, he might as well work on the fraud case that he'd been given. Dees was still pissed that Jack had so easily relinquished the case he was working on to a coworker, which only made Jack even angrier.

But if he wanted to stay an FBI agent, all he could do now was return to Memphis, even though he had no idea how he was supposed to focus on that while the whole situation with Wyatt was going on. Though he trusted the other agents in his sector, he didn't like the idea of being so far from Valentina until the guy was officially arrested.

With a frustrated grunt, he realized that all he could really do now was to bring Valentina up to speed and to tell her to stay away from Wyatt until his arrest, so he called her home phone. After a couple of minutes though, she still hadn't picked up. The phone kept going straight to voicemail.

Panic immediately started to course through Jack's body as he kept dialing her number again and again, every time with no answer.

"Where the hell is she?" he muttered while shoving the phone in his pocket, already rushing to the office's entrance. He quickly grabbed his things and Valentina's cellphone before running out.

To hell with Memphis, he thought, frantically fishing the car keys out of his pocket.

He jumped in the car and headed straight onto the highway toward Long Lakes, regretting never asking Valentina for any of her friends' phone numbers. Jack tried his best to stay calm, to repeat to himself that she was probably just out for a walk or maybe she was with Michelle at the general store, but the fear of something happening to her quickly killed those rational thoughts. Maybe Wyatt knew of Jack's suspicions and had decided to take action before Jack could stop him.

With that idea in his mind, he pumped the gas harder. He usually was a very careful driver, but at that moment, he used every bit of the defensive driving training he'd gotten at Quantico as he pushed his speed to ninety. He didn't care about the speed limit or anything else. All he cared about was getting back to her before it was too late, if it wasn't already…

He pushed the limits of his training, driving frantically, weaving between cars, burning through red lights and stop signs. As he drove, he kept calling her, and every time he heard that damn voicemail, he felt a little more dread pooling in his stomach. By then, it'd been hours. If she was out, she would have been back by now, right?

Jack started to punch in another call to her when a car suddenly swerved into his lane. He slammed on the brakes. The tires squealed underneath him, and he braced himself, expecting to hear the sickening crunch of metal upon metal.

He laid on the horn. "Asshole!" he muttered as the car came to a shuddering stop. He took a deep breath and the man in the other car gave him the finger and sped off.

Hours later, he finally pulled into the entrance of the Long Lakes development. He tore down the residential road, hardly feeling the bumps of the potholes underneath him, raising a whirlwind of dust all around the car. When he pulled in front of Valentina's house, he jumped out and knocked on the door.

No answer. Inside, the dogs barked. He peered through the side window, but could only see them, jumping up to meet him.

Turning around, he looked up and down the street. Her car was in the drive. *Something's wrong.*

Jumping back into his car, he rushed to Michelle's.

He kept knocking and knocking at her door, but she wasn't home either. Maybe they were together? Worried sick, he backtracked and headed for John's place.

John opened the door with a benevolent smile. "Oh, hello, and—"

"I'm looking for Valentina. Do you know where she is?" he blurted, breathless.

"I am afraid I do not. What is the matter? Did something happen?" he asked, inspecting Jack, who had sweat stains under his armpits and a crazed look in his eyes, noting he was red-faced and short of breath, like he'd been running a marathon.

"I don't have time to explain. If you see her, tell her to call me immediately!" Jack yelled while running back to his car. He drove to the general store, the adrenaline pumping through his veins. The only other time he'd ever felt so panicked and afraid was when he and Valentina almost died because of that damn drug business. He couldn't help feeling like this was all his fault.

After that incident, he'd hoped he would never feel like that again and yet, here he was, with his heart beating so hard he could almost feel it exploding through his chest.

"I failed," he said aloud to himself. "I failed, and now she's dead."

Out of desperation, he hit the steering wheel so hard with the heel of his hand that pain rocketed up to his elbow.

Jack skidded to a stop front of the general store without even taking the time to park the car. He left it idling in the middle of the parking lot and jumped out to run into the store, not bothering to slam the door shut.

Ellie gave him a puzzled look.

"Jack, are you okay? No offense, hon, but you look terrible."

Frantic, he ignored her, his eyes darted around the place, until he saw Valentina and Michelle sitting at one of the corner tables, chit-chatting and laughing.

He let out a long breath. He felt so relieved to see that she was okay that all that adrenaline left him at once and he nearly collapsed to his knees.

"Jack! What the hell? You'll scare all the customers, fella," Ellie shouted, making Valentina and Michelle turn. Valentina immediately ran to him, and Michelle followed.

"Jack? Are you okay? What happened?"

He hugged her tight.

"I was so worried about you," he said, leaning his head on her shoulder, breathing in her sweet smell.

"What do you mean? What's going on? You're scaring me."

"We should get out of here," Michelle suggested, noticing Ellie and all the other patrons staring at them.

They went out to the parking lot and Jack leaned against his car, trying to calm down. Valentina stayed right next to him, with a supporting hand on his arm.

"Can you tell me what all this is about?" she asked again.

Jack quickly glanced at Michelle, realizing that the fewer people who knew about this the better; otherwise, the rumor of Wyatt being a murderer would have quickly made its way to every single person in the community, not only spreading panic but also giving Wyatt a chance to avoid arrest.

"Can we talk about it at home?"

Valentina nodded and looked apologetically at Michelle, who nodded sympathetically. "You two take Jack's car back. I'll drive up later, after I've picked up a few things at the store. Let me know if you guys need anything," she said, giving Jack a worried look as she headed back inside the store.

"Thank you, Michelle." The two of them got into Jack's car.

As soon as he put the car intro drive, Valentina said, "So, tell me what that was all about. I'm assuming the cell phone uncovered something?"

He nodded.

"What? Is it bad?"

"It was Wyatt, Val," he said, "He had a tracking device on your phone. He's been surveilling you. I'm pretty sure he was the one who killed that woman who lived nearby."

Eyes like saucers, Valentina looked at him incredulously.

"I… I don't understand…"

"Think about it. Why else would he put that app on your phone? He had to have a reason to."

"You know for sure it was him? Why couldn't it have been—"

"It was him, all right. I'm sure of it."

"How… How do you even know this?"

He told her about the articles that he had found regarding the other murder in L.A. and about all the connections that he was able to make.

"You were going to be next," he said, his voice cracking up. "I'm sure of it."

She gasped. "Why would you even think that?"

"Because. It all makes sense. Him coming around, checking out your phone. He was priming you. He was checking out your house so that he could come in later, and murder you. He's a sick son of a bitch."

Her mouth hung open. "I don't—I don't believe it."

"You know, people thought the same thing about Ted Bundy—he was too charming to be a killer. But it's true. He's a manipulative, charming murderer who takes advantage of lonely women. That's why I was so scared when you didn't pick up the phone at home. I thought he'd already gotten to you."

Valentina didn't say anything, she just sat there, staring absently at the road in front of them, her hand tight around the door's handle. "I still don't understand. Why me?"

Jack shrugged. "He's just sick. Sometimes there is no other reason."

She shuddered visibly. "But he has it all. He's a famous movie star. I never thought—"

"Yeah. I know." He stared out into the trees, wondering if Wyatt had been the one snooping around in them, peering in windows. If he had been tracking other women, too. If he was responsible for other murders, in other places. Who knew what else he was capable of? Sick people like that simply couldn't stop killing. It was an obsession.

"Are you sure about all this?" she murmured after a while.

Jack nodded, putting a comforting hand on her leg. "I know it's frightening. Hard to believe. But you have to trust me on this. Val, I am so, so sorry."

She bit her bottom lip and her eyes got watery because of the tears that she was trying to hold back.

"I let him into my house," she said, visibly shaken. "I made him dinner. I kayaked with him. And I was alone with him, so that at any time—oh, God. I could be dead right now."

She buried her face in her hands.

"He's methodical. Takes his time. He wants to make sure no one else will suspect him."

When she pulled her hands away from her face, tears fell down her cheeks. "You were right about everything. I'm such an idiot…"

"No, hey, you couldn't know, okay? The important thing is that you are fine and the FBI guys are coming to arrest him. Everything is going to be all right and I won't leave your side until this is over, I promise." *Even if it means losing my job. This is more important.*

Jack held her hand tight until they got back to her house.

Valentina went straight to the back porch and sat on her double Adirondack chair, staring at the lake. He made her a cup of tea and brought it out to her.

"I thought this might help you feel better," he said.

She barely smiled at him, accepting the cup. He sat down next to her, putting an arm around her shoulder to try and comfort her.

"I'm sorry I didn't listen to you," she said.

"It doesn't matter, Val. What matters is that you're safe."

He kissed her on the head and she leaned against him, still looking absently at the water as Jack held her tighter, thinking that it was true: all that mattered was her. He knew that, after disobeying his boss, there was a very good chance that he would be fired, but somehow that was completely unimportant to him right now. It was better not to tell Valentina about the argument he had at the office. There was no need to stress her even further.

And maybe it was a good thing, if he lost his job. He and Valentina would be together, permanently. Maybe he could put into effect a plan to live out here for good, get a less stressful job in town. Something.

They spent the rest of the afternoon on the porch, trying to keep themselves occupied with reading, though Jack, at least, couldn't keep his mind on his book. He kept thinking about the case, and what Dees and the rest of the homicide unit were doing with the local police.

"When will we know about the arrest?" she asked after a while. She was clearly having the same troubles he was.

"I'm not sure," Jack said, "But let's not talk about this."

At dinnertime, they went inside. Jack decided he'd fix a light meal for Valentina, even though food was the last thing on his mind.

"I think I'll just go to bed," Valentina said when she saw him getting some food out of the fridge.

"Nonsense. You gotta eat something."

She reluctantly agreed, so they sat down and ate, immersed in an awkward and heavy silence, without even enjoying the beauty of the sunset turning the lake's waters a bright pink color.

Barely an hour later, while they were lying together in bed, she whispered to him, "Thank you for always being there for me."

"Of course," he whispered back.

After that, Jack noticed that she kept tossing and turning. He wanted to stay up with her until she could finally fall asleep, but he was exhausted, and drifted off into some very disturbing dreams, about a sick person, roaming the woods, peering in windows, watching them all.

Nineteen

When Wyatt woke up that morning, he had a bad feeling rooted deep in his stomach, a feeling too strong to be ignored. He slowly rose to sitting, staring at the one ray of sun that was able to sneak in through one of the heavy curtains of the big bedroom window.

With a grunt, he stretched, waiting for sleep's bleariness to slowly fade away. Then he quickly showered and headed into the kitchen for breakfast. Still the feeling kept nagging at him. He was so focused on it that he forgot he had put a couple of eggs on the stove and almost burned them.

All morning he tried to shake that feeling away, to convince himself that he was just being paranoid. Valentina's boyfriend wasn't after him. Melissa's murder would never get pinned on him. He had been following the news very carefully, trying his best to make sure that nobody connected him to it. Between that and having to spy on Valentina to make sure her boyfriend wasn't getting any ideas, his nights mostly consisted of staring at the ceiling, or tossing and turning. For the past few nights, he'd been resorting to drugs to help him sleep. Though they worked, they made him drowsy and lazy for the rest of the day. Lately, he'd barely gotten out of the house.

He was going crazy. Living this double life was too exhausting. On the surface, he was this famous, charming actor who had everything going for him. But there was this dark side to him, a side that he couldn't quite shake.

More than once he'd been tempted to contact his lawyer, to tell him everything, but he always backed out. This suffering was no worse than having David lecture him, or whatever the consequences of his actions were going to be. He was already suffering, here, because of it, locked up in this house, missing his extravagant L.A. life.

Wyatt grabbed his computer to go through Valentina's phone once again when he heard a loud, insistent knock on the door. He instantly froze with one hand on his laptop. His eyes locked on the door while he waited, in absolute silence, for whoever it was to go away.

When he heard a second knock, even louder than the first, he jumped; that bad feeling was now digging a pit in his stomach. It was only when he heard a man on the other side yell: "Mr. Rogers, this is the FBI, open up!" that his knees gave up on him for a second and he had to grab onto a chair to avoid collapsing.

Shit. They weren't going to go away. The knocking kept getting louder and the voice more impatient as the agent kept calling his name. They knew. Somehow, they knew… He hadn't been careful enough, and now there was nowhere to run. His eyes darted about frantically, looking for some escape.

"Mr. Rogers! We know you're in there. Open the door or we'll have to bust it down!"

Wyatt took a deep breath and, his hands slightly shaking, he did his best to not look completely panicked while he took very slow steps toward the door. The moment he opened up, ready to try to calm the agents down with his charm, one of them jumped on him, knocking him to the ground.

"What the hell?" he was barely able to say, as the air quickly left his lungs because his chest was now pressed all the way against the hard wooden floor, just like his face was. The agent who tackled him was incredibly heavy, twisting his arm with a force that Wyatt was surprised didn't dislocate his shoulder.

In the meantime, a couple of agents stayed next to him, pointing their guns down while the rest searched the house and yelled stuff that he didn't understand. They were talking about finding weapons and he had no idea why. What weapons did they think they were going to find in there?

"Let me up…" he tried to say again, only to have the agent atop him twist his arm even harder.

When the other agents were done making sure the place was secure, they presented him with a search and arrest warrant he was too upset to even understand. Then they took his laptop, his phone and all the newspapers regarding the murder near Long Lakes that he had piled up on the kitchen's counter. They took nearly every last thing that belonged to him, much to Wyatt's confusion. What, exactly, did they need his toiletry bag for?

Finally, the agent that had knocked him to the floor grabbed him by both arms and shuffled him to standing. As he got up, a sharp pain scissored through his back.

"What the hell is going on?" he yelled. "Do you really need to use such brutality? My lawyer—"

"Mr. Rogers, you are under arrest for the murder…"

He heard nothing else. Murder. It took a moment for the word to sink in. He felt like he was in his old life, playing a part, this time of a wanted criminal. But then he realized this was real life, his life, and they were talking about him. He needed to respond with something, not just open-mouthed shock. Indignation, at the very least.

Finally, the words came: "What? What are you talking about? I didn't kill anybody!"

The words came in and out of his head. "You have the right to remain silent; anything you say can and will be used against you in a court of law…"

Wyatt didn't hear any more after that. He yelled at the agents to let him go, that there had to have been some mistake. He put on the best performance of his life, one that would've won him an Oscar in Hollywood. This one was the one that counted most.

Even after they sat him in one of the cars, with the handcuffs too cold and too tight around his wrists, he kept yelling that they had no idea who they were messing with, that all of those accusations were ridiculous and that he had some very powerful friends and would get them all fired. No one seemed to hear his screams and threats. Eventually he leaned against the seat, silent, sweat beading on his brow.

He'd been arrested for murder. This would make it around the world in seconds, knowing how fast bad news travelled. Likely, David already knew about it.

They drove him across the state. The whole time, the officers in the car refused to answer his questions. His mind whirled. On what grounds were they accusing him of murder? Was it because somebody was able to connect him to Melissa? Even if that was the case though, they couldn't have any proof that it was him, could they? They couldn't just go there and arrest him. He needed to talk to David. He wouldn't say a goddamn thing until he was there.

Later, inside a cold interrogation room at Nashville's FBI headquarters, Wyatt stared at the metal table in front of him, waiting for somebody to come in and clarify the accusations against him. He kept tapping his foot nervously and sweating profusely despite the air conditioning. Finally, a tall man with a beard and a chubby guy came into the room and sat in front of him, shoving some files and documents in the middle of the table, together with the newspapers that were taken from his house.

"I have been waiting here forever," Wyatt started. "I need to talk to my lawyer. I get accused of murder and nobody tells me where these ridiculous accusations even come from!"

The shorter agent glanced at his colleague with an irritating smile on his face and the tall one, in a calm manner, crossed his hands on the table, looking at Wyatt with a serious expression.

"Mr. Rogers, I'm Agent Smith and this is my partner, Agent Williams. Since you seem so confused about the accusations against you, let me clarify things, eh?"

"You'd better. If this is about that girl, Melissa, I was with her, yeah. One night. But then, I ended things. So if you got my DNA from there, it doesn't prove anything."

Ignoring that, Agent Smith opened one of the files, taking out some pictures. They showed two dead women lying in unnatural, twisted positions on the floor, as if they were weird raggedy dolls just tossed to the ground. Their eyes were wide open in terror, bright red marks on their necks, their tongues horribly swollen and sticking out of their mouths.

Two women. Wyatt quickly looked away, disgusted by the images. He was able to recognize them both, of course. Melissa was the woman he spent that one night with, and Camille was the girl he'd dated for a little while back in L.A., the one who worked on set with him.

"I'm sure you recognize these two women," the agent said.

He tilted his face to the ceiling. "Get those pictures away, please… I need to talk to my lawyer."

Smith put the pictures back in the folder, never taking his eyes off Wyatt.

"Did you know these women?" the other agent asked in the raspy voice of a heavy smoker.

"Yes… I… well… I knew Camille, we… uh… we dated for a short time. We were supposed to go on vacation together but then I never heard anything from her, she didn't show up at the airport and she never returned any of my calls. I just figured that she changed her mind or something. I had no idea that she was dead, I swear."

"And you didn't think to check on her?"

"I… no…To be honest, I didn't really care that much…"

One of the agents nodded.

"I didn't…" Wyatt was about to say but he got interrupted.

"What was your relationship with the other woman, Ms. Covington?"

"There wasn't one! I told you! One night. We had dinner together once and that was it. It was a one-night stand, I didn't have any reason to kill her, or Camille," he repeated. "Look. I've said enough. I need to talk to my lawyer."

The two men exchanged a look, as if he was already guilty. They ignored his request. One of them leaned forward.

"So, it's just a coincidence that these two women, who both had a sexual relationship with you and who lived two thousand miles away from each other, were both strangled to death in a very similar fashion?"

He stared at them, astonished. How could that be? "I don't understand it."

"So you don't have any explanation?"

"How could I? I didn't do it!"

"So you deny having anything to do with these murders, despite your close involvement with both women?"

"Yes!" Wyatt barked. "Unequivocally!"

Again, the two agents exchanged a look and Wyatt felt helpless. His breath became labored.

"And what about the fact that both their security systems were hacked and that they both knew their killers? That a coincidence too?"

Hell. They did? This wasn't going well. "I don't know. All I know is—"

"We know about your studies at the University of Tennessee, Mister Rogers, and we also know that, before becoming an actor, you were thinking about a career as an electrical engineer, and that you had some IT classes, as well. So you had some technical ability, huh?"

"That doesn't prove anything," Wyatt fidgeted on the chair, drumming his fingers on the cold metal of the table, unable to stay still. He wished he could run as far away from there as possible.

But he'd done that already. He'd run away, to avoid everything. If the wilds of Tennessee weren't remote enough, where else could he go?

"Maybe, but you'll have to admit that we're talking about a lot of coincidences here," Smith pointed out, leaning in close as if he was just waiting for Wyatt to crack under his pressure.

"How do you explain that both these women were murdered in the same exact way, while in a relationship with you?" Williams asked.

"I just said. I don't have an explanation; I don't know who is doing this or why, but I swear that it wasn't me. What would my motive even be?"

"That's what we are trying to figure out, here. Sometimes, there isn't a motive. Sometimes, sick people kill for the pure joy of it." Smith grinned a little sadistically. "Is that you?"

He shook his head. "Of course not! I'm not some sicko."

Smith opened another folder, showing him a list of data and codes.

"This is the code for the spy app that you installed on Ms. Bianco's phone, isn't it?"

Ms. Bianco. Valentina.

Oh, shit. They knew about that? Wyatt stared at it, feeling even worse than before.

"Could you explain why you planted this? Was Ms. Bianco going to be your next victim?"

He fisted his hands in his thick hair. "That has nothing to do with any of this nonsense!"

Smith leaned against the chair, a self-satisfied smile on his face, crossing his arms in front of his chest.

"Would you care to enlighten us, then? Because it's pretty damn suspicious how you began spying on this woman. Why else would you do that unless you had some interest in her?"

He nodded. Even he had to admit, it looked bad. If he were on their side of the table, he'd probably think the same.

"Okay, listen. At first, I was only trying to pass the time, just like with Ms. Covington. I wasn't actually interested in a relationship with either of them. Country girls… They're not for me," he cleared his throat, tried to keep his cool, he still hoped that they would see that it was all a huge misunderstanding, "Then I was told that Valentina's boyfriend worked for the FBI's fraud squad, and I got afraid that, maybe, he was going to figure out my tax evasion. *Tax evasion.* That's what I thought you were arresting me for. Not murder."

The two agents kept listening to him, piercing him with their eyes while a fat drop of sweat ran down his temple.

"So I put that spy app on Valentina's phone to keep track of her boyfriend's moves. I know that what I did was wrong but I was just trying to look out for myself, I would never hurt anybody."

"We'll be the judges of that, Mr. Rogers."

Williams pushed the newspapers toward him.

"You were really interested in the investigation of Ms. Covington's murder, weren't you? I wonder why."

Again, Wyatt squirmed on the chair before replying. "It's true, I followed the case. I was worried about something like this happening, actually. I thought that if somebody saw me with her or figured out that we'd been acquainted I might have become a suspect or somebody would have wanted to ask questions. But not because I was a murderer. I was worried about my tax evasion, so I didn't want any unnecessary attention. That's the whole reason why I came to Tennessee in the first place."

After that, they asked him to provide an alibi for the dates and times of the murders, but in both cases he'd been home alone. The thought hit him then—if he'd just listened to David and done what he was supposed to do, which was stay out of sight, he wouldn't have met Melissa, and he probably wouldn't be in this position in the first place.

David was right. Shit. He couldn't wait to hear David gloat about that one.

Well, screw it. He'd *let* David gloat, as much as he wanted, if he could be a good attorney and get him the hell out of this.

At the end of that interrogation, which seemed to drag on forever, the agents did not seem convinced of his innocence at all, and his nerves were shot.

"I want my lawyer now!" he mumbled, beaten. "I'm done being accused of crimes that I didn't commit!"

"Oh, calling your lawyer is definitely going to be a good idea."

He was left alone again until two other agents escorted him to a phone. He called David, who, as expected, went apeshit and kept cursing at him over the phone but agreed to be on the next plane out. Then he was brought to a cell where he was told he would have to stay until his lawyer arrived. And who knew how long that would take? Knowing David, he'd probably let Wyatt dangle a little, just as a "I told you so," and to prove how important he was.

In the cell, Wyatt stared at the wall, feeling numb and exhausted.

Was he really going to end up in prison for the rest of his life? No, he was Wyatt Rogers, the famous movie star, and the world made exceptions for people like him.

David would get him out of this. He just had to sit tight.

Twenty

Absently petting Dante from her Adirondack chair on the back porch of her house, Valentina watched the ducks making ripples upon the placid lake. Thoughts of Wyatt jarred her, all the seemingly innocent interactions she'd had with him cycling through her head in a never-ending loop.

For the past few days she hadn't been able to stop thinking about Wyatt's arrest. Now, alone, as she glanced over at Firefly Cabin, she shuddered. It was too close to home.

Again.

Jack had gone back to Memphis; he'd explained to her that he didn't want to test his boss's patience more than he already had, and he'd also assured her that she was safe, now that Wyatt was in jail. Though Wyatt hadn't admitted to the murder, he had admitted to tax fraud or something, and Jack seemed convinced it was only a matter of time before the FBI wrangled a confession out of him for the murders.

Despite all that, Valentina couldn't shake the unsettling feeling that had plagued her from the moment Jack told her about Wyatt spying on her. Learning that he'd been planning to kill her for absolutely no reason didn't help. Not only that, it brought back all those horrible memories from a couple of months back.

Wyatt Rogers was a sick man. As nice and charming as he'd been to her, he was a killer. He murdered for the sheer pleasure of it.

A chill slipped its way down her spine as she thought of the handsome actor. He'd had millions of fans, and yet he'd fooled them all.

Certainly, none of them suspected that Wyatt Rogers was a psychopathic serial killer with a blood lust, capable of murdering women so easily.

Even now she shook her head in disbelief. The picture in her mind was so incongruous with the man she'd met.

Her train of thoughts was interrupted by her home phone ringing. She got up to answer, and Michelle's voice instantly relaxed her.

"I just wanted to check on you," she explained. "Are you all right?"

Michelle was the only one who knew about what had happened with Wyatt because Valentina had told her about it. Of course, inevitably, the rumor mill that had already been churning with the arrival of Wyatt Rogers in Long Lakes immediately went into overdrive at the not-so-subtle appearance of the FBI at the actor's rented cabin. Now everybody knew at least some details (whether or not they were accurate seemed beside the point), and Valentina didn't feel like going out or seeing anybody.

"Thank goodness. I thought you were Lola. She's been calling me non-stop, wanting the dirt."

Michelle let out an exasperated sigh. "I am sure she has been. She cornered me in the general store yesterday, asking about you. Seems the whole town wants to know. So tell me."

"I'm fine, I guess…" she answered, even if she was very well aware that she couldn't lie to her friend that easily.

"You seem doubtful." There was a brief pause before Michelle talked again. "What if I came over tonight? Now that Jack's left, I'm sure you need some company."

Valentina massaged her forehead, feeling the tightness in her muscles; she'd recently been tormented by sharp migraines that worsened her mood.

"Oh, but don't you have to pack for your trip with John?"

"No, I have plenty of time for that!"

Valentina finally admitted, "I don't know, Michelle. I don't think

I feel like entertaining."

"Nonsense! I'll entertain *you*. I'll bring you something nice to eat. We'll drink some wine, maybe watch a movie and get your mind off of everything."

"Okay, okay, you win," she gave up, finding herself smiling. She wasn't in the right mood for dinner –she'd had no appetite ever since the news about Wyatt—but Michelle was right. She could use some company and a distraction.

"Awesome! I'll see you around seven?"

"Seven works. I'll see you later."

"Later!"

Normally, Valentina would wear some nice clothes to have dinner with her friend. Nothing fancy but something a bit better than her usual casual or sporty clothes, but this time she didn't feel like changing. When Michelle knocked at the door, later that night, Valentina greeted her in a plain T-shirt, sweatpants and dark circles under her eyes. Michelle probably noticed it but didn't say anything. Instead, she gave Valentina her brightest smile. Michelle prepared an omelet with vegetables and its inviting smell made Valentina feel a little bit better. They sat down at the table, the dogs resting at their feet and a bottle of wine to share.

"I still can't believe how naïve I was, Michelle," Valentina exclaimed after a while.

Michelle gave her a compassionate look. "Don't be too hard on yourself, hon. How could you have known? Besides, I think he fooled pretty much all of us. I hear Lola's fast-tracking that petition so we'll get more security in, and she's also now promoting a second petition so that we require background checks of all temporary residents."

Valentina nervously tapped on the table with her finger, wondering if that would have even helped. After all, Wyatt Rogers could have probably charmed his way out of a background check. He was just that good. She was about to say that when the dogs sprang up, facing the front door, growling menacingly. The two women immediately turned to the commotion, confused. All looked normal, but

Valentina was used to her dogs sensing things she couldn't.

"What's got into them?" Michelle asked.

"I have no idea. They probably smell an animal or something. Let me go check."

The moment Valentina got up, the dogs ran to the door. She grabbed their collars, struggling to keep them inside while they impatiently pushed and beat their tails against her legs.

"Calm down you two!"

Squinting in the darkness that swallowed the perimeter of the house, she looked around. At first, she didn't see anything. Then, out of the corner of her eye, she spied a quick movement near a grove of trees at the side of the house. She turned in that direction trying to make out the shape as the sound of crunching leaves and twigs rose up. She could have sworn she saw the shadow lurking behind the trees.

Valentina, you're just being paranoid because of what happened, she thought, dismissing it with a sigh. *It's probably just your doe and her adorable fawns who came back hoping for a little extra treat.*

Closing the door tight, she went back to the kitchen island, where Michelle was holding her wine glass, frozen. "What was it?"

"Oh nothing. Just deer, I think."

"Are you sure? Maybe it was that Long Lakes creeper."

Valentina shook her head. "That was just a rumor. Or maybe that was Wyatt. Whatever it is, it shouldn't bother us anymore."

Michelle nodded, taking another sip of wine. "Let's hope so! So how long will Jack be gone now?"

"Probably for a couple of weeks at least. He was working on a case prior to all this, and didn't know if the other agent had made any progress with it while he was gone."

"I see. Thank God he decided to come back."

"Yeah, thank God," Valentina murmured, trying her best not to show how frustrated she was with herself for not listening to Jack from the very beginning. He was an FBI agent, *per la miseria!* He had an instinct for this kind of stuff, the same instinct that had saved her in the past. How could she have not trusted him right away after he'd proven to her what he was capable of? And if he hadn't insisted on taking her phone to check it out, she might've been dead by now.

A shiver ran down her spine as those thoughts cluttered her mind once again. Michelle must have noticed, because she took her friend's hands in her own.

"Valentina, listen, I know this is tough, but I also know that you're strong enough to get over it, eventually. The important thing is that nothing bad happened to you and that you're safe. Soon Jack will be back and you'll be able to enjoy your time together."

Valentina forced a smile while Michelle's words resonated in her head: *The important thing is that you're safe*. Those were the same words that Jack kept repeating to her as well. She couldn't help but think about how ironic it was that, even in a remote, idyllic place like Long Lakes, safety was not to be taken for granted.

"How about we talk about you and John, instead?" she said to change the subject.

Michelle immediately blushed, waving her hand as if she was trying to keep an annoying insect away. "There is nothing to talk about."

"Oh, please. You two are always spending time together now, and you planned that vacation."

Michelle smiled, nodding.

"Yes. It is so nice to be with him. He's so kind, Valentina, and so funny. And he never runs out of interesting stories to tell me."

"Of that, I am sure. You're going to have a great time together."

They laughed and, after finishing dinner, they quickly cleaned up before sitting on the couch to watch a movie.

It was pretty late by the time Michelle left. As she left, Valentina thanked her again for dinner.

"Don't mention it," Michelle said, giving her a quick hug. "And please, if there is ever anything I can do for you, I'm only a phone call away!"

Before going back inside, Valentina scanned the darkness around her cabin. She crossed her arms to keep from shivering, suddenly gripped by the distinct, unsettling feeling that someone was watching her. But nothing was visible through the thick darkness of the forest. She shook her head and stepped inside.

I need to stop doing this to myself, she murmured to herself, closing the door and locking it, then throwing the deadbolt, just to be safe. *It's over. Everything is okay now.*

After that, she climbed the stairs and took her time getting ready for bed, knowing that sleep would not come easily. She was right; she kept tossing and turning, but hours later, she finally felt drowsy enough to drift off.

It was a sound echoing through the house that woke her up. She looked at the bedside clock and discovered that it was after one. She stared at the bedroom's door, listening, wondering what was going on. Was it the dogs? Heart thudding in her chest, she waited for the sound to come again. Silence.

Maybe I imagined it.

Still, she knew she wouldn't be able to fall asleep without at least checking. So with a grunt, she swung her legs over the side of the bed and got up to check, dragging her feet toward the staircase.

"Dante? Luna?" she called as she reached the foot of the stairs.

Despite the fact that she was still slightly dizzy from waking up so abruptly, she quickly realized that something was off: her dogs weren't inside. They were barking *from the outside.*

What's going on? she thought, carefully making her way down the steps. *Was I so tired last night that I forgot to let the dogs back in the house?*

She was about to open the door, confused, when she felt a movement behind her. Icy tendrils of fear pricked at her neck.

She didn't have the time to turn because somebody wrapped something around her neck so tightly that the air suddenly escaped her lungs. The shock gripped her. Someone… in the house… choking her. Her entire body started to shake in fear as her hands jolted up to find the piece of cloth tight around her throat.

This wasn't happening. The killer had been caught. She was

imagining this…

But the explosion of pain in her chest told her that this was no nightmare.

"Please…" Valentina was able to whisper with a raspy voice, "stop…"

But whoever was doing this clearly had no intention of stopping. Her assailant tightened the grip on her neck even more to the point where she could feel herself getting dizzy, her vision swimming as her eyes bulged. Her heart was beating so fast that it hurt and her shaking hands were loosening their grip on whatever was around her throat, something rough tearing painfully at her skin. Tears streamed down her cheeks as she faced death once again. Only this time, nobody was there to save her. This time, there was no question.

She was going to die.

That was the last thought her brain was able to process before everything went dark.

Twenty-One

It had been a long day. John finished dinner and stood at the sink, doing the dishes, while Sherlock rubbed up against his leg, purring. As he placed the last dish in the rack, he looked outside the kitchen window, admiring the shadows of the trees standing tall in the darkness. He decided to sit on the porch for a couple of minutes to enjoy the night's cool air.

Of course, Sherlock followed him outside to jump on his lap while he slowly rocked back and forward on his antique chair, the one that he had brought there from his old house in England. It was strange to think about how quickly time passed, about how many things had changed since he'd moved to America.

His thoughts ran to Michelle. He would have never expected or hoped to find such a connection with a woman at his age.

Certainly, he would have been fine with only the company of his loyal cat, but it was so nice to have somebody like her to spend time with, talking about each other's lives, discovering how much they had in common. It definitely had been a nice surprise.

After sitting there for a little bit, he almost fell asleep, so he decided to go back inside, where he went about his normal night-time routine before climbing into bed.

He was long asleep when something suddenly landed on his stomach, jolting him awake. Opening his eyes, dazed and confused, he blinked to focus and spotted Sherlock in the shadows, mewling softly.

"What are you doing, boy?" he murmured, propping himself up

on his elbows, watching the cat now sitting on the window's sill. Sherlock was usually just as lazy as he was and rarely roamed at night. This time, however, there was something different. The cat was nervously swinging his tail from side to side, staring curiously out the window.

John got up to stroke the cat.

"What is it?" he asked, knowing that any strange behavior in his cat usually meant that something was off. The cat didn't answer, obviously, but John stared in the same direction, pulling the blinds up.

He squinted in the darkness, expecting to spot the dark outline of a coyote or raccoon or other creature of nature, rambling through his yard. But he didn't even see that. He also thought about the Long Lakes creeper that Michelle had spoken about, but he felt for sure that that was only a figment of the imaginations of some of the strong personalities that lived in this place. This window faced the home of Valentina, but her house was dark. All seemed normal.

That is, until he listened more carefully. He heard dogs, barking in the distance.

"Bloody hell! Those dogs are going insane."

It could only be Valentina's dogs and yet those lovely creatures were usually extremely well behaved and had never barked like that in the short time he'd been there. Plus, he knew that Valentina kept them inside at night, and it sounded like they were outside.

What, exactly, were they doing outside? It was too late for them to be out. He strained to see them, but couldn't make out their shapes. In the dark night, everything was completely still. Everything seemed all right.

And yet Valentina's dogs were out, and going crazy.

Something was wrong. He could feel it. It was a thing he'd learned from all of his investigations—a little tickle on the back of his neck. Even the smallest of feelings could mean something big.

He had to check it out.

"Wait here, Sherlock," he said as he quickly put on his robe and a pair of slippers. "I need to see what's happening at Valentina's house."

The cat just stared at him, still swinging his tail from the windowsill. John rushed down the stairs and out into the night, walking as fast as he could while the gravel crunched under every step. The house wasn't very far away, but it wasn't in view until he crested the hill. When it did come into view, though, it seemed normal—quiet, the lights out. Still, the closer he got to the house, the stronger that bad feeling got.

Once he reached Valentina's driveway and the porch came into view, he realized that he was right: the dogs were outside, barking and howling at the door, scraping it with their paws. Whatever was happening inside, it clearly wasn't anything good. When the dogs saw him, they rushed across the lawn to him, jumping on him so excitedly that they nearly knocked him to the ground.

"Oh, my, it's okay, it's okay," he whispered, patting them on the head before lightly nudging them aside and continuing to the front porch, his slippers growing wet in the dewy grass.

He listened at the door, hearing muffled noises. Carefully he nudged the door open, but the dogs excitedly flew ahead of him, throwing the door wide open.

As his eyes adjusted to the darkness, he gasped at what he saw. The dogs were snarling and barking at a figure that had been backed up against the corner of the living room, while Valentina's body lay motionless on the ground.

"Damn dogs!" the attacker yelled as one of the dogs fastened its jaws around the assailant's arm. The attacker let go of the leash they were holding.

It was at that moment that John recognized the person standing there: it was Taylor, the dog sitter that Michelle had introduced him to. Despite the shock, before she was able to make another move, he grabbed a bottle of wine that was sitting on the kitchen counter and swiftly smashed it against Taylor's head.

The crash was incredibly loud as she fell to the floor right next to Valentina, pieces of shattered glass and wine raining down around them.

Breathing heavily, his hands shaking, he reached for Valentina. He knelt next to her, struggling to keep the dogs away as they tried to sniff and lick her, and checked her pulse. It was extremely weak, but still there. He noticed her phone on the counter and grabbed it to call an ambulance.

"Nine one one, what's your emergency?"

He was in such an agitated state that he could barely bring himself to speak. Finally, he barked out the words, "Please, I need an ambulance. A woman has been strangled."

Once the ambulance and the police had been called, he went through the phone to find Jack's number. The phone rang but nobody answered, so John called Michelle instead, who appeared in the door minutes later.

"What if the ambulance doesn't get here in time?" Michelle asked, her voice shaking while she held Valentina's hand.

"I'm sure they will, my dear. Don't worry."

Michelle sobbed while John promptly and skillfully tied up Taylor with the same leash that she'd used to try to kill Valentina. Valentina was still alive, but unconscious.

"I don't understand... Why would she do this? Why would anybody do this?"

John shook his head, rubbing her shoulder and staring at the pretty young girl tied up on the floor. She looked so sweet, so innocent, and the last time he'd met her, he'd thought what a lovely girl she was. How wrong he had been. Why would she want Valentina dead?

It seemed like an eternity but, finally, both the ambulance and the police arrived. They worked on Valentina before putting her onto a stretcher. "Is she going to be all right?" Michelle asked as the EMT wheeled her out.

"We'll do everything we can, Ma'am," was his terse reply.

Taylor had moved or mumbled something a couple of times but never fully regained consciousness. The police cuffed her and loaded her on a stretcher to be taken to the hospital for her injuries. A couple of officers stayed with John and Michelle to get their statements and to understand what exactly had happened there.

"I just don't understand why she would want Valentina dead. They barely knew each other," Michelle said, still trembling in John's arms. "I was the one who introduced them... She seemed like such a nice girl. I... I really don't understand."

She started crying again, and John consoled her by rubbing her back gently. "It's all right. You couldn't have known."

"Ma'am," said the police officer, "as soon as Ms. Miller wakes up, we'll do our best to get to the bottom of this. And I am sure that Ms. Bianco will recover in no time."

Michelle and John nodded as the officer told them that they had been extremely helpful and should now try to get some rest. Instead, they stayed up for the rest of the night at John's place. They tried to call Jack again but he never answered, and Michelle was too shaken to be left by herself. John made her some tea that she barely sipped, and they fell asleep in his 221B apartment in the basement of his house, in the comfortable tufted leather chairs around the fireplace, as the sun started to rise above the trees.

Twenty-Two

Jack slowly opened his eyes. The headache from all the beers he had drunk the night before rapidly flushed through his temples as his lips curled into a grimace. Once he was back in Memphis, he'd met with Franklin Watts, the guy who was assigned to him, to discuss any possible progress on his part, which wasn't much. Then Franklin had invited him out for a couple of drinks, on him. He probably figured that was the best way to get Jack on his good side after stepping into his investigation like that.

Franklin had turned out to be pretty all right, actually, and Jack ended up enjoying those free drinks maybe a little bit too much. At least, that's what the headache was telling him right now as he lay in bed, not wanting to get up, after his alarm clock went off.

With a grunt, he leaned on his elbow and turned the alarm clock off. Just then, he saw that he had multiple missed calls from Valentina and a couple of messages from numbers he didn't recognize in his voicemail.

Suddenly, he was wide awake. It must've been pretty late when she'd called. She never stayed up late unless she had Michelle over for dinner, and even then, she didn't usually call him.

He let out a curse. How could he have missed her calls?

Maybe she's just on edge because of what happened with Wyatt, he told himself as he pressed the voicemail button. The voice wasn't Valentina's though. It was a man's voice. It sounded familiar but he could not make out who it was. The only thing he was able to register was that there had been some sort of incident.

"This is John Watson," the voice finally said, as he made the connection. It was a British accent. Suddenly, everything became clear. Valentina's neighbor. For reasons still unclear, Michelle's pet sitter, Taylor, had tried to kill Valentina the night before. Luckily, John was able to prevent any tragedy from happening and now, both Valentina and Taylor were in hospital, their condition stable.

"What the…" he murmured to himself, hardly able to believe the words. It felt like some cruel trick. She'd been in danger. Without him. Again.

Jack clutched his phone so hard that he heard a cracking sound. John had left other messages, but Jack was so furious in that moment that he didn't think about listening to those just yet. Instead, he got up, punched the wall so hard that his knuckles started to bleed and a small crack formed on the spot he just hit. Why was this woman trying to kill Valentina? Did she have anything to do with Wyatt? Maybe they were accomplices? Did she go after Valentina as revenge against him?

His first instinct was to run. To get there as soon as possible. But where was *there*? What hospital? He put his hands in his hair, trying to breathe in and out properly, trying to calm down. Pacing the room, he listened to the other messages. According to John, Valentina had woken up a couple of times but was too out of it to speak of what had happened. She just asked about her daughter before losing consciousness again but the doctors said that physically she was fine. They were going to keep her under observation for a couple of days just in case, but all she needed was some rest. Taylor, on the other hand, had to get stitches and was refusing to cooperate now that she was in custody.

Jack could not believe that all of that happened in the short amount of time he had been back in Memphis and he could not believe that, after all he had done, he still hadn't been able to protect Valentina. It took him a good minute before all that frustration and anger dissipated enough for him to think lucidly again. There was no question that he would have to go back to Long Lakes immediately, but there was something else that he needed to take care of before that.

Jack dressed quickly and packed an overnight bag, then headed to the airport. He looked at his watch while in line for the check-in as he rang up Bruce Dees.

"Jack," his boss exclaimed when he finally picked up. "I heard about what happened. I am so sorry."

Jack bit his lip, annoyed that everyone had heard about it before him. *Damn, I should've been there.* "How did you—"

"The FBI is there in Long Lakes right now, investigating any connections it might have to the other murders in L.A.. They have reason to believe that woman, Taylor, might actually be from California, too. And that she might have been obsessed with that actor, Rogers."

"About that, sir. I would like to assist in this girl's interrogation."

There was a pause on the other side.

"I don't know, Jack…"

"Come on. It's my girlfriend. I deserve this opportunity!"

A couple of people turned to him and he lowered his voice.

"Please," he repeated.

His boss sighed. "I'm not making any promises. Maybe, if you get there right away. They're not going to wait."

"Thank you," Jack said before hanging up.

The normally quick flight was excruciatingly long. All he could think about was Valentina. Valentina hadn't answered any of his calls, and it was driving him insane not to be able to talk to her. There were just too many unanswered questions swirling in his head.

The moment his plane landed, though, all those questions disappeared and his only focus was to see Valentina as soon as possible. He rented a car and went straight to Cookeville's hospital. The entire drive, despite what John had told him about her being fine, he could not help but picture the worst. The thought made him press even harder on the accelerator.

The drive to the hospital seemed endless, but Jack finally pulled up at the front of it, parking haphazardly in the first spot he could find. He rushed inside, yelling like a mad person for someone to tell him where she was.

A sympathetic nurse guided him to one of the rooms, saying that she was stable but heavily sedated, and couldn't have visitors for too long. He nodded, then slowly walked into the room, sighing with relief on seeing that, beside a horrible bruise on her neck, she seemed fine, even if it wasn't pretty to see all those drips attached to her. The feeling of remorse and guilt got stronger once he was in front of her. She was awake, her eyes were faraway, closing from time to time. There was a lot of light coming through the room's big window and, despite the circumstances, she looked so peaceful, but fragile at the same time. An empty tray was resting on a small table in front of the bed and next to it there were some flowers in small, pretty vases, most likely from Michelle.

"Hey, Val," he said sweetly and she opened her eyes completely. The moment she saw him, she started crying and he hugged her as tight as he could, mindful of the IV line. After a little bit, Jack pulled away from her to look more closely, caressing her hair gently, mindful of her injuries.

"How are you feeling?" he asked after she calmed down, but she only shook her head.

"I'm so glad you're here," she whispered instead in an unrecognizably raspy voice.

"Me too. I'm so sorry, I had no idea this would happen… After Wyatt's arrest, I thought… I thought…"

She shook her head again. "I don't want to talk about this."

"Okay, I understand."

She relaxed in his arms.

"Have you called Bea yet?"

"No, I didn't want to worry her. I was going to wait until I felt… until I was… better."

He kissed her forehead.

"After this, I am going to meet with the FBI. I need to see the woman who did this to you."

Valentina immediately became stiff. "Do you really have to?"

"I do, Val. I need to understand."

"Your colleagues can just tell you about it, though."

This time, he was the one shaking his head. "I need to hear it from her."

"If you say so…"

He smiled. "Yeah. Believe me. I'm used to dealing with tough subjects. Maybe not murderers, but people who commit fraud can be surprisingly violent, too. Trust me. It'll be all right."

Tears leaked from her eyes. She started to speak, but nothing came out.

"Hey, hey, hey," he said, moving in closer. "If you really don't want me to, I don't have to. I just—"

"No. It's not that. It's just—I'm so glad you're here." Now a tear really did fall down her cheek. "Like I said, I couldn't tell Bea, or anyone else—but you're here. And I'm so glad."

He leaned over and wiped the tear from her cheek, wondering how he'd ever doubted her love for him. Of course she loved him. Of course he was the only man in her life. It was evident in everything she did and said. He felt silly for ever thinking otherwise.

Valentina didn't say anything else after that and the nurse came back, asking Jack to leave.

"I'll be back after the interrogation. I promise."

Again, Valentina didn't say anything. She barely returned the kiss that he gave her, but he knew that she simply needed some time to process what Taylor had done to her.

Jack was feeling pretty tired. After all, it had been a long day, most of which was spent sitting in the car in the middle of the traffic, but he was finally there. With a cup of coffee in his hand and one of his friends from work by his side, he stood on the other side of the interrogation room's glass. He didn't even really need that coffee; all the adrenaline that got into him after seeing Taylor enter the room was enough. But Louie insisted.

The girl looked very different from the first time he'd met her. She had deep circles under her eyes, a wild look in her eyes and her hair was dirty and pulled up in a lopsided ponytail. Now she didn't look like any average college student trying to make some money on the side. She looked like the psychopath that she was.

Taylor was clearly agitated, but kept her stubborn facade up for almost an entire hour before she finally started to give up information. Jack knew one of the guys interrogating her—Drew Terrisson. He knew that if somebody could get even the toughest criminal to talk, it was Terrisson, so he knew this wisp of a girl wouldn't last under the pressure.

"Taylor. Is there any relationship between you and Mr. Rogers? Were you trying to hurt Ms. Bianco for him?"

Yes, Jack was wondering that too. After he first had that idea, he thought it was kind of far-fetched, there was no way an actor and a pet sitter had anything in common and yet, there must have been something that Terrisson knew. Otherwise he wouldn't have asked that question.

Taylor started laughing. "You could say that."

"What do you mean?"

For a second, she stopped talking to stare at the glass and Jack wondered if, somehow, she could feel his presence there. She shrugged and Terrisson hit the table with his fist, making her jump.

"We are not here to play games, Taylor. I want to know why you attacked Ms. Bianco. Was it a vendetta of some sort? We know from your personal database that you and Mr. Rogers studied at the same university. Was he in contact with you? Did he ask you to do this?"

Taylor fidgeted tensely, her leg bouncing up and down, looking everywhere but at the two agents in front of her.

"Nobody asked me to do anything," she finally answered.

Jack was now so close to the glass that he could almost touch it with the tip of his nose.

"But I did it for him anyway. I love him!"

She sounded very hysterical now, smiling eerily and dreamily like a girl in a romance movie.

"I love him, I love him, I love him! And I would never have let anybody get between us. He loves me too! I know he does!"

"Taylor, calm down!"

Taylor yanked the handcuffs that were holding her wrists, then she rested her head against the table, sobbing.

"Jesus," Louie commented, sipping the coffee that he got for himself, "girl sounds pretty messed up to me."

"Shhh! I want to hear."

"Wyatt and I dated, back in college," Taylor went on explaining. "And I knew he was my soulmate. But then he got into acting, became famous and never kept in contact with me."

She leaned forward. "See, he used to be different back then. He wasn't as sophisticated as he is now but I never cared. And then he changed. He became this famous movie star. But that's not who he was. I knew, if I just gave him a little time, he'd come back to me. So I kept tabs on him. I always made sure to know where he was or what he was doing. That's why I came to Long Lakes, so that I could be with him."

"How did you know about his trip to Tennessee? Only his agent and the man who rented him the place knew his whereabouts."

Jack now found himself leaning completely against the glass. Dees was right: he wasn't a homicide detective but he would have given anything right now to be the one interrogating her. Taylor shrugged, until Terrisson insisted on her answering the question.

"Fine," she said finally. "I've been stalking him for years. He might have been taking classes in IT, but so was I, and I was better at cybersecurity. It made it extremely easy to spy on Wyatt without him realizing anything. I'd go through his social media, emails and texts. I knew everything about his personal life. I was even aware of the tax fraud he recently committed. I thought about using that against him, but that wouldn't have gotten rid of the bitches who tried to take him away from me. Besides, it was also just as easy to break into their houses to kill them."

She spoke of it like it was nothing, as if she had no remorse at all and would do it again if given the chance. Jack's grip on his cup of coffee tensed while Louie kept shaking his head in disbelief. Like him, Louie was a fraud agent, and he wasn't used to seeing dangerous criminals go off like that.

"Ms. Bianco never dated Mr. Harrison though," the detective said after she calmed down a little bit.

"He was getting interested in her. He asked her out," Taylor murmured, her face twisted in hate.

"So you broke into her house and tried to kill her."

"Yes…"

Terrisson and his partner nodded, looking at each other, then gathered their documents and left the room to join Jack and Louie.

"Well," Terrisson said, "Full confession. She won't get out of jail any time soon. If her lawyer doesn't decide to plead insanity."

Jack turned to him. "That won't happen. That'd be a waste of time."

"It usually is because it's a hard thing to prove, but it turns out that Miss Crazy Pants here might fit the bill. She has a record of full psychotic episodes going back to her youth. That's why she grew this insane obsession over Rogers. The jury might actually go for it."

There was silence for a moment before Jack left the room to go sit at his desk. He hid his face in his hands until he felt a gentle nudge of his shoulder.

"You're all right there, Bud?" Louie asked, and Jack shook his head.

"I just want that crazy woman behind bars. We'll all be safer that way."

A couple of people turned to look at him but he didn't care. He didn't care about anything except making sure Taylor would pay for her crimes—and being looked after in a secure psychiatric hospital didn't seem to fit the bill. She'd destroyed two lives, and had tried to destroy Valentina's. A hospital seemed too good for her.

"It's just a possibility, Jack. Maybe it won't work. It often doesn't. And even if it does, she'll be locked up in an institution for the rest of her life."

Jack nodded but his friend's words didn't really help. He needed to focus on the fact that at least they had a full confession and now they knew why she'd done it. .

Later that afternoon, when it was almost night, Jack went back to the hospital to keep Valentina company. She was still very weak and not very talkative. She asked him only why Taylor tried to kill her but didn't want to talk about what happened beyond that.

Jack, despite being worried about Taylor's trial, was exhausted. He soon fell asleep on a chair next to Valentina's bed. He woke up for a couple of minutes in the middle of the night and saw that she was holding his hand in her sleep. He caressed it, leaning with his head against the bed, feeling so frustrated with himself once again. He had been so sure that Wyatt was the killer that he didn't even try to think about who else could have been doing this and he knew, deep inside, that it was his own jealousy that had blinded him.

If he had acted the right way, if he had tried to be more rational, maybe, just maybe, things would have played differently and Valentina wouldn't have had her life put at risk again. He wondered whether she might have been better off without him around. He kissed her on the forehead before falling asleep again, praying that Taylor would end up in prison for almost taking Valentina away from him.

Twenty-Three

It was a very warm day, sunny and with a clear blue sky, not a cloud in sight.

A perfect day to go home.

The doctors had thought that the shock could have put her health at risk, so they'd insisted on her spending at least a couple more days under observation. At first she'd made a fuss about it. She'd felt fine and didn't like the nurses hovering over her and checking her every two minutes like mother hens. But Jack persuaded her to listen to the doctors and to rest before going back to Long Lakes.

Truthfully, it hadn't taken much. Even now, the thought of going back to the place where she'd almost died filled her with dread. But now, three days after she'd been brought to the hospital it was time to finally go home and try to put all those horrible moments behind her.

"Mom, how are you feeling?" Bea asked her worriedly, helping her out of the wheelchair as Jack pulled the car to the front of the hospital.

"I'm fine. Stop babying me," she said to her daughter, smoothing the girl's dark hair as she stood and hugged her. "I'm the mother and should be babying you."

The pretty girl's eyes were wide with worry. "But—"

"It's final, *tesoro.* Jack will take it from here. I'll be in very good hands. You need to get back to school. You've already missed too many classes!"

She sighed. "I've only missed a couple days. It's—"

"Go!"

She pulled her daughter into a hug and whispered a goodbye in her ear. She hated goodbyes with Bea, and didn't want to drag it out. She was still in a fragile state and couldn't be sure she'd be able to keep the tears from flowing.

"Call me tonight! Goodbye, Jack!" Bea said, rushing across the street to the parking lot and her car as Jack came around and helped Valentina into the passenger seat.

He settled in being the steering wheel and looked at her. "All right?"

She nodded. "I think so."

Valentina relaxed against the seat, looking outside of the window as Jack's car jolted at every bump in the road. Now, he was finally bringing her home.

She turned towards Jack, who was silent and focused on the road. She'd asked him not to talk about Taylor's interrogation or upcoming trial but she knew he really wanted to. He didn't have to say it; she could tell by the way his expression changed and a crinkle appeared over his eyes whenever his thoughts wandered there. Once, he mentioned that it was because the judge might send her to a psychiatric hospital instead of a prison and he simply could not let that go. Valentina didn't care. Being alive and knowing that, either way, Taylor wasn't going to hurt anybody else, was enough.

"I'm sure you need to be heading back, too," she said, finally. "You've missed a lot of time, as well, taking care of me."

He shook his head. "No need."

She studied him, trying to decide if he really meant it, or if he was just trying to shield her from the troubles in his job. "But I know that job in Memphis is a bear, and—"

"It's over."

She blinked. "It is?"

He nodded. "Turns out, being here in Long Lakes had been good for me. The second I had some time to relax and think about it, I remembered what had been evading me all this time."

She stared, astonished. "And what is that?"

"You see, I kept investigating the managing director because he was the only one who knew about the Saudi Arabian fund wanting to buy a substantial share of that stock, but I never thought about the other person who knew about it, because she was sort of a hidden figure."

"Who was it, then?" Valentina asked, her curiosity now piqued.

"His secretary." Jack laughed. "I would never have figured that out, but when my colleague made a totally casual remark about how pretty the secretary was and wondered whether she was having an affair with the director, since she spent an awful amount of time in his office, the light bulb just went off in my head."

"Because she could hear everything he said," Valentina said, impressed.

"Not only that. She was the one who carried out his orders and asked the brokers to carry out the transactions. She had all the details."

"So she was buying shares for herself right before the stock's value increased due to the Saudi Arabian fund buying such a large share?" Valentina was no financial expert, but that definitely sounded suspicious.

"Actually no. The first thing the SEC and I did was investigate all the employees, and they were all clean. But she was leaking privileged information to an ex-boyfriend, a small-time independent broker who lives in Boston. He bought the shares and they split the dividends."

"How did you find out about the boyfriend?"

"Once I realized who the insider trader was, it was a just matter of what we call 'carrot and stick' questioning. The stick being a long jail sentence and the carrot being a more lenient one if she revealed her accomplice's name. Easy peasy."

"What's going to happen to Memphis Brokerage now?"

"The whole account is going to prosecution, and Bret Copland is in heaps of trouble, although it wasn't technically his fault. Not that I feel sorry for him; the guy was nothing short of insufferable and uncooperative, and probably should've noticed something was amiss himself. I knew I'd smelled something rotten."

"Of course you did! You're great at what you do!"

"So anyway, no rush. I'm here if you need me."

That was the best news she'd heard in a long time. Valentina grabbed Jack's hand and he turned to smile at her. She also knew how responsible he felt for what had happened, even though nobody could have ever imagined that Taylor was a cold-blooded serial killer. She sighed, leaning her head back, enjoying the air coming from the open window.

Finally her house appeared in front of her eyes and, as soon as Jack stopped the car, she jumped out and rushed toward the entrance, already hearing Dante and Luna barking from the inside. The moment she opened the door, her dogs jumped on her, wagging their tails and licking her hands so she kneeled down to hug them. Jack waited behind her, smiling, then helped her get up.

"I'm going to take a shower," she told him.

He nodded. "Need help?"

She laughed. "Nice try."

As she walked toward the bathroom, she tried her best to ignore the shivers she felt when flashbacks of Taylor sliding the leash around her throat crept into her mind. She had to take a couple of deep breaths in order to cross the living room area without getting short of breath. She quickly grabbed some clean clothes from the bedroom and closed the bathroom door behind herself. It was such a relief to be able to shower at her own place. The only thing that really worried her was spending time there without Jack. He was here now, but eventually he would have to go back. The idea of staying alone in the house was now upsetting, but what choice did she have?

Relax, Val. He's here with you, now, and that's what matters.

"I'm going to call my colleague tomorrow," Jack told her when she got out of the bathroom with her hair still dripping water on her shoulders. "I'm going to pick the best alarm system ever created."

She smiled at him, grateful, even if she would have rather had him there instead of a new system. This experience had certainly taught her never to underestimate the importance of a good alarm, no matter where she lived.

"How expensive do you think that'll be?"

He shrugged his shoulders, "It doesn't matter, Val. I can help you cover the expenses and I know this guy well. I'm sure he'll make a special deal for me."

She nodded, tightening the towel around herself, getting lost in her thoughts once again.

"You're okay?"

Valentina nodded again but didn't say anything. She was just standing there, her eyes pointed toward the window but completely absent. Jack walked to her to hug her and she breathed in the comforting smell of his cologne.

"It's going to be all right," he murmured against her hair, "It's just difficult right now but it will all be okay. I promise."

She returned the hug, hoping that he was right. "I'm just glad that you are here," she said honestly, making a mental note never to take a single moment of it for granted.

Epilogue

One week later, Jack and Valentina went to Michelle's place for dinner. She'd been visiting Valentina almost every day to lift her spirits, often bringing her some delicious products from her garden, trying to convince her to come over. Valentina kept making excuses, but gradually she was beginning to realize that she couldn't hide in her home forever, and could definitely use the distraction. She was starting to get used to being in her house again, but the first few days had been horrible. She couldn't sleep because she jumped at every single noise, constantly looked behind her, even during the day, sometimes without even realizing that she was doing it, and she'd lost much of her appetite. Plus, the pain killers that the doctor prescribed her for the injuries made her stomach upset. The idea of spending some time with her friends, enjoying Michelle's delicious food, was certainly welcome.

"Are you sure you feel like going?" Jack asked her for the hundredth time that day. Ever concerned about her welfare, he'd been suggesting they just stay at home and relax in front of a movie.

"I'm okay. I promise."

She put on her most convincing smile and he kissed her hand before opening the car's door for her.

"I'm sure that Michelle will understand," he'd told her at breakfast, but Valentina was determined to do this. It was a warm night and Michelle had set the table outside on a back porch with a view of the lake, very similar to Valentina's. John was there, too, and he hugged Valentina as soon as she walked onto the porch.

"My dear!" he exclaimed, "I'm so relieved to see that you're finally up and walking."

"All because of you, John. I'll never be able to thank you enough," she replied, holding his time-weathered hands in hers, and gazing gratefully at him. "You know, that bottle you used to attack Taylor was actually a very rare vintage that I was saving to celebrate Jack's success with Wyatt's case."

His eyes went wide. "Oh, I'm sorry, my dear… How expensive was it?"

"You don't want to know, trust me! But it definitely wasn't worth as much as my life."

John nodded, still holding her hands, then Jack cleared his throat and asked Michelle what they were going to have for dinner.

"I made some lasagna. I hope it will pass the Italian's judgment."

Michelle winked at Valentina, who laughed as her friend motioned for her to sit down.

"What will happen to that actor, now?" John asked Jack, who was about to sit next to Valentina.

"Most likely he'll just get a hefty fine. He's all over the newspapers, but you know what they say. There's no such thing as bad publicity," Jack grumbled.

"So he was not involved with Taylor, whatsoever?" Michelle asked.

Jack shook his head before explaining that Wyatt denied any type of involvement.

"When Wyatt was asked about her," Jack carried on, "He barely remembered who she was. Apparently, to him, she was just a fling, hardly more than a one-night stand from his college days. It's crazy to think about how strong her delusions about him were. She definitely has some mental health issues."

John and Michelle were listening with a captivated look in their eyes while Valentina kept her eyes on her lap. As much as she didn't want to hear about it, she'd heard bits and pieces from the case here and there, enough to patch together the complete story.

"It's unbelievable," Michelle commented, "Taylor seemed such a nice girl. We all trusted her with our pets. I can't help but feel responsible for all of this."

"Michelle, what nonsense is this?" Valentina finally intervened. "How could you be responsible?"

She shook her head sadly. "I was the one who introduced you to her."

"You couldn't have known," John reassured her, "Nobody could have. Well… except for Sherlock, of course. He knew right away! He never liked her. And he was the one that sensed there was something wrong at Valentina's that night. He's really the one who saved the day, once again."

The others tried their best not to laugh at John's theory and Valentina already felt a bit better.

"I'm sure he did. He's a very special cat," Michelle said, holding John's hand before getting up to take the lasagna out of the oven.

The food was delicious and the night extremely pleasant. The topic of Taylor was soon dropped. Valentina still had that bad feeling crawling under her skin but, just like she'd hoped, her friends helped her feel like she could go on with her life.

Seeing her daughter in the hospital and now spending time with her friends and Jack was what she needed to remind herself not to give up and to remember that she was surrounded by people who loved her and were there for her. Also, soon, Jack's colleague was going to install that new alarm system which, hopefully, would give her more reassurance. The only thought that she couldn't shake though was that, despite how idyllic a place like Long Lakes looked, it gave a false sense of security, leading people to think that nothing bad could ever happen.

But deep down, she knew the truth was quite different: *Nowhere* was ever really safe.

THE END

Acknowledgments

This book, more than others, has been a fantastic team effort. I could never have done it without the great people who collaborated on this project.

The first person I want to thank is my amazing daughter Costanza Garassino. Without you, the ideas that whirled inside my brain during my hikes would have never found a way of escaping the hard walls of my thick skull and flowing onto printed paper. One day, you will become an outstanding writer . . . just wait and see!

The other stunning members of my team are, once again, Cyn Balog and Jayne Lewis, the two most awesome editors that an author could ever wish for. You are the ones who created order from chaos, and that's no small feat. A special thank you to Bonnie Salem and Federico Rivalta. You helped me navigate the turbulent waters of financial fraud like the pros you are.

As usual, I want to thank you, the Reader, for choosing to spend your time reading my book. I hope I have kept you good company and that this is only the beginning of our travels together. Ciao!

Antonella L.M. Rivalta

Antonella L.M. Rivalta is a full-time translator and localization specialist but, as soon as she clocks out of her day job, she shifts gears and writes gripping romantic suspense novels. Born and raised in Milano, Italy, three years ago Antonella decided to take the leap from Italy to the United States, along with her perplexed husband, culture-shocked daughter, two stoic dogs and a very sullen cat. After settling in a beautiful gated community in the Tennessee woods, she immediately decided to follow her heart's pull and start writing the action-packed thriller novels that slowly but steadily take shape in her head during her long hikes. Her own experiences in adjusting to such a vastly different culture are a constant source of inspiration for the Long Lakes series' main character, Valentina.

When she is not burning the midnight oil writing her next novel, Antonella spends her free time reading, looking for hard-to-find ingredients for her Italian dishes, walking her two Collies and traveling the USA in her RV. An outdoor enthusiast, she enjoys mountain biking and hiking in the Smokies. For more information about Antonella and her books, visit www.antonellarivalta.com.

Books By This Author

Elsewhere

Behind the gates lies a secluded community with secrets to die for . . .

The idyllic gated community of Long Lakes, Tennessee, is the perfect location for Italian-born Valentina Bianco to start over after her painful divorce. Except the town isn't the quiet refuge she thinks it is.

Undercover FBI agent Jack Erikson doesn't know what to make of the fiery, outspoken beauty he encounters at the general store. He can't afford to get on the wrong side of the locals while he's investigating a suspected fraud and is determined to win Valentina over.

Valentina can't deny the spark between her and Jack, but she senses there's more to Jack than his easy-going nature. Together, they're in danger of exposing a dark underbelly of lies and deceit running deep beneath the entire community that's far deadlier than fraud.

And whoever is behind those secrets is prepared to kill to keep them quiet . . .

www.ingramcontent.com/pod-product-compliance
Lightning Source LLC
Chambersburg PA
CBHW060455300726
48975CB00008B/2526